Doctor Flesh: Director's Cut

By Alex S. Johnson

And Spewed Upon The Firmament From:

MorbidBookS.

Everything
Bleeds.

Morbidbooks Is A Grotesque Bizarro Ballet Where The Most Profane Things Occur. An Impious And Perverse Dwelling Of Dark Revulsion. A Cozy Cottage Where Torture Porn And Brutal Bible Tales Are Devised. A Quiet Place To Relax And Spin Tales Of Depravity And Wickedness. A Halfway House For The Disturbed Where Rules No Longer Apply. A Safe Haven For Deviant Serial Killers To Hatch Their Wretched Schemes. Bring Your Pets. The Tasty Ones Are Always Welcome.

HTTPS://WWW.MORBIDBOOKS.WORDPRESS.COM

"I shall set down in a few lines how uptight Maldoror was during his early years, when he lived happy. There: done. He later perceived he was born wicked: strange mischance! For a great many years he concealed his character as best he could; but in the end, because this effort was not natural to him, each day the blood would rush to his head until, unable any longer to bear such a life, he hurled himself resolutely into a career of evil ... sweet atmosphere!"

Comte de Lautréamon, *Maldoror*

ACKNOWLEDGEMENTS:

"Doctor Flesh: Nude for Trankenstein" originally appeared in somewhat different form as a 25-copy limited edition chapbook from Dynatox Ministries, published by Jordan Krall.

"Blood Ties" originally appeared in the *Deathmongers* anthology, edited by Robert Friedrich.

"Bangkok Gunfighter Without Pointless Huck Finn" originally appeared on the *Strange Edge* blog, edited by G. Arthur Brown

"Mr. Sugar Comes to Splatterville" originally appeared on the *Cease, Cows* blog, edited by Heather Nelson

Front and back cover credits: Photography and concept by KC Focht Musser. Digital manipulation: Alex S. Johnson. Model: Lora Bloom. Venue: Eris Temple Arts, Philadelphia, PA.

Doctor Flesh: Director's Cut is dedicated to the fine folks in the Clown Horror Anthology chat on Facebook.

Special thanks to RE Davis for his help with formatting fuckery.

Alex S. Johnson

Table of Contents:

Doctor Flesh: Nude for Trankenstein

I.

Return with us now to the bump n' grindcore in progress. The girls twitch and moan on their respective racks, exuding trickles of sweet juice. Meanwhile, Viola plummets through porous ceilings on her way to an encounter with a pair of legs clad in peppermint stick stockings and an ass marvelous to behold and fondle. She slides an ungloved hand between the legs and brings her fingers back to her mouth. The fragrance of fear and desire makes her dizzy. The girl's upper body is jammed into what appears to be deep blue sky or perhaps a foam replica of same.

Stationed at random intervals at the entrances and exits to Viola's virtual labyrinth are a fake Catholic school girl, an actual crone and an intermediary who shuffles between them with infinite patience and slowness and is constantly getting in the way. The last time Viola jacked out, the school girl followed her back into the warehouse laboratory and appeared on occasion either as an erotic apparition or as a warning that the crone was somewhere in the vicinity. The crone's pink hair had the texture of a Brillo pad and a slightly soapy feel. Viola could see the crone coming towards her, followed by the intermediary, who doubtless bore one of a thousand indecipherable messages relating the adventures of the fake school girl. At a certain point Viola Flesh simply pushed the girl through a block of utility fog which held her like a bug in amber unless the intermediary, whose name was Mel, released her with a wand resembling a Fourth of July sparkler.

After consulting the appropriate passages in the Key of Solomon, Viola sits down in front of the editing bay, wearing the rubber body suit with studded fingertips. From the speakers overhead pour "Another Liddell Piece of My Heart" by Lewis Carroll Overdrive. The transdermal patch on her forehead pulses, pouring the trance medium through her blood. She places her hands palm down on the foam pad and slots the studs into metal cups, waits as the data streams connect

Entering the darkfield, her body caressed by thousands of signals. They feel like tiny pinpricks erupting from a sheath of velvet cloth. The connection is made as a throbbing sensation begins in the base of her skull.

The lab machines sing her a lullaby as stars smear across her vision. Gradually she feels her core separate from the body. The stars make flourishes and arabesques like the tracery of glowsticks. The darkfield splits and she sees her body on the other side as the invisible wall seals it off from view.

A brief spike of panic as she feels all the molecules in her body loosen like a cloud of pollen and float in the void. Then, gradually, they collect again as her astral double—or whatever the hell it is—solidifies.

She hits the jungle floor silent as a Ninja, inhaling the fragrance of the flowers and the musky scents of the animals that prowl her creation.

***

Dr. Viola Flesh: celebrity narcissist, proxy mutant or original genius? For nearly everybody outside her circle, the jury is out. At the risk of hubris, she allows herself the best possible spin on an admittedly messy identity. As she sits in her own private jury box she listens to the testimony, still unclear exactly who they're babbling about. At least for once the voices are outside her head.

In a somewhat objective arena she's right on the cusp of unveiling her new invention, for a limited audience at first: Beta-testers, some hand-selected (the blogger, Bilge), the majority randomly chosen by her mule, Solare.

Solare's gender is a mystery. One of the few successes—the term is provisional—sprung from Dr. Flesh's early work. As a mule, Solare has been extremely effective in abduction, subtle mind-fucking and other, more inscrutable tasks unknown even to itself. The mule's ignorance works in Flesh's favor.

Even Viola doesn't know what to call the new thing, the prototype, the Object to Destroy Heart-Shaped Brides. The working term she uses is Reality Stack, but the bloggers have already circulated the meme of "fuck/shit stack," and Viola's backers can taste her blood, almost literally. The rumors trickling through the Supranet indicate that Dr. Flesh has "lost what's left of her freaking mind" (Fanbloggia.com), "retired her sanity—if she ever had any" (Boringcrap.com) or "convinced herself once again that she is the love child of Leni Riefenstahl and Andy Warhol—which she ain't" (Bittergeeks.com).

Most of her previous innovations have been both extremely dangerous and far too bizarre for commercial use. A team of lawyers has been working around the clock to suppress victims of the Stack's precursor from venting their displeasure. Enormous sums have been administered, strong-arm tactics used as a last resort.

Admittedly, Viola's unorthodox blend of science, black magic and avant-garde cinema had created casualties, limping creatures whose dark hearts and minds were consumed with endless vengeance. Even Viola, whose very cells crawled at the idea of her own culpability, had to come clean on this point. After all, victimhood was something she regarded with an icy, Promethean disdain. Too close to home, too much like Oklahoma, the Drama Club, bullying, the dreaded Two Hole Punch, secret dreams of

Family Bondage icon Val Valentine, and a pronounced taste for filmy, silky underthings (or were they underlings?)

And an obscure pumpkin-based metaphysics. She could feel their presence now, her orange nemeses, carving themselves into jagged-tooth grotesques only she understood. The pumpkins had suggested that last project, Not Quite a Reality Stack But Darn Close, the beta audience for which had been transformed into Shamanic Druids with shaky hands and a penchant for outré vegetable sports.

Yes, her earlier experiments had yielded victims, but NQRSBDC was not to be blamed solely. She would not yield on this one qualifier, although her lawyers had suggested that this was the whole point. Cinema remained for her a pure art form, with all the perils inherent therein. In the words of another practitioner, you bought the ticket and took the ride. Had she not herself submitted her sanity to the jaws of madness, the perilous orange fear that drove her to the brink of reality TV, and even beyond? Besides, nobody had put a gun to anybody's head and forced them to participate.

Actually, this was not quite true. The gun was of a decent caliber and many of the heads still bore the impress of its barrel. But the principle remained. Movies weren't responsible for madness, death, dismemberment, the sudden urge to emulate a great horde of Sodomy Mimes and inject one's self with the Dream Liquid, or to rage naked in the streets with prophesies of the last days, when the pumpkin horde would come to visit and stay to teach the malformed ontology of puppet-fucking.

(Or would they?)

Viola looked fondly across the warehouse at the upright coffin that housed Solare. The she/he/it embodied everything Viola loved: the glamorous ooze of androgyny, the seeping carnage dispensed nightly to Viola's foes. Even its peculiar need for cookies took on its own charm under full moonlight. She thought she could hear it munching in there right about now, the sounds resonating through the naked pipes that ran up and across the ceiling, raising dust on the floorboards and a species of red army ant. So simple were its basic needs, and yet so complex a personality she had rarely known. Without Solare, she would be left with a private hell, with nothing to shield her from the pumpkins.

Maybe it was asleep, dreaming of Amsterdam and sloppy, nameless holes.

"Solare, can you hear me?" she asked.

Silence.

"Don't be impertinent," she said, her tender feelings shaded with irritation. Lately, Solare had developed an attitude and probably needed a hypnotic upgrade. Or downgrade. Or a head-butting. Or a cheese-grating.

"I summon and succor thee by all the powers of Pokemon, wake and show thyself."

Petulant silence.

"Don't make me come over there," said Dr. Flesh firmly. "I have a mission for you."

"Come out and kill for Mistress?" said Solare in its smooth, mellow voice.

"In a way," said Dr. Flesh.

"No."

Viola sighed. It was time to make use of the stocks, the hypodermic, the shock therapy and direct anal injection of fuzzy worm bile.

She picked up the coil up the coil of wire and experimentally squeezed the alligator-clip electrode attachment.

"I guess you'll miss out on the fresh batch of cookies I just had delivered," she said. "Too bad. They sure look tasty."

She heard movement from the coffin. The lid slowly opened.

"Cookies?"

***

The unincorporated area just south of Noe, where Bunuel Avenue and Fulci Street briefly merged and the wrong side of the tracks peeled back in a Moebius striptease to become the full tracks, was a virtual No Man's Land. This was outlaw territory, where surreal things happened to absurdist people.

With sufficient perspective, you could see the point where the garment district halted abruptly and fled in abject terror, where the sweatshops curled up like the paws of imaginary roadkill, and all but the sketchiest felt a bone-deep sense that past this boundary line, all bets were off.

Those traits that made SoNoe anathema to the nice and normal were precisely why Viola had chosen it. Here, if their instincts for self-preservation were intact, they left you alone. Even the ghetto birds stopped circling here, as if they had hit an invisible wall. The sidewalks crackled with fissures, and the glowing eyes of the mutated wrecks that lived beneath could be seen even in daylight.

Of course, there were some disadvantages to living and working in SoNoe. Insurance agents wouldn't set foot there on a dare. If a building burned to the ground, it stayed burnt, a grim reminder that some laws were not meant to be violated.

Nevertheless, for one bent on meme-morphs and the construction of soft machines, the area had a definite bent appeal. It was a place where the sight of an oiled, nude hermaphrodite thumping down the street, its head encased in an arcane harness, barely registered. Nor would anyone think to call the authorities when an absurdly tall woman in a leather bustier, black PVC skirt, fishnet stockings and stiletto heels equipped with actual stilettos, armed with a tranquilizer gun and with a psychotic gleam in her eyes, sped down the sidewalk in hot pursuit. In SoNoe, you left well enough alone. That was the price of freedom.

"Don't make me use this," Viola bellowed. Five feet ahead of her, Solare had stopped in its tracks, coughing and grunting. It turned around and shot Viola a defiant middle finger.

"Oh, we're playing Gingerbread Man now, are we?" asked Viola.

"Sarcasm...will get you nowhere," said Solare, its voice muffled by the harness. "I'm sick and tired of being your guinea pig, your test subject, your ass-worm host."

"Headset a little too tight?"

"See, that's what I'm talking about. You treat me like a thing. I am a human being, not an animal. I have feelings and thoughts. Surely you can recognize that."

"Of course," said Viola in a wheedling tone. "I know that. Your humanity was never in question. But I thought we had an agreement. A contract."

Solare fought for breath. "One second," it wheezed. "Boy, I really do need to exercise more." Sweat was streaming down its flanks.

"Why don't you come back to the lab," said Viola, "and I'll try to make a slab a little more comfy. I promise."

"Okay, okay," said Solare. "I'm sorry I ran out like that. It was the insects. I...I couldn't take the bug shot."

"Bug shot?"

"You...have no idea how uncomfortable that is. One hundred live centipedes playing nano-chess in your intestines? And they weren't even following the rules. Half of them were cheating. And that—it tickles. It tickles bad."

"I promise I will extract the insects," said Viola. "Let's get you back to the lab, ok? I can't do surgery here."

Solare sighed and slumped its shoulders, defeated.

"Okay," it said. "But there better be cookies."

"All you can eat," said Viola. "I promise."

***

Nathan Hale Bilge, administrator, architect and chief staffer at Psychogremlin.com, licks the potato chip crust from his fingers and readies himself for another plunge into the cybernetic fray. He truly loves his work.

"Dr. Flesh has a certain cachet among shithuffers and doomdoorbellringers," Bilge writes, enjoying his own wit, "although personally I've never understood what all the fuss is about. *Evil Ass III* was a disappointment on just about every level, even as conceptual art. So far, all this auteur has managed is to raise one's gorge. Fandom cannot embrace her pretensions without the onset of severe brain atrophy, the general public won't touch her, and the mainstream critics have so far eschewed her work. Yesterday I received an invitation to her new piece, *Reality Stack* I have to admit I'm curious, despite my misgivings and skepticism about her talent. If nothing else, it should be good for a few laughs."

Bilge's fingers hum like tiny engines. One final push, and he's through.

"With any luck, *Reality Stack*'s reception will convince Dr. Flesh to stay in the lab where she belongs, producing questionable inventions, the utility of which has never been clear."

He kisses his fingers and clicks "publish."

II.

"I'm bored," whined Solare from the depths of the coffin. "May I come out and kill, Mistress Mommy?"

"Have some more cookies," said Dr. Flesh. "Mistress is working."

This was the contrary nature of the beast. When she needed it to abduct and render, it got whiney, but when she needed to focus on something, it wanted to come out and kill for Mistress.

She had tried several times to recode its hypnotic patterns, but the thing was developing an annoying will of its own. And the fuzzy worm bile just made it horny. So that was out.

"Okay," said Solare. But it was a petulant "okay."

A few minutes later, Viola spun away from the computer, stood up and began pacing the loft.

This was no way to live. Keeping Solare in cookies was not a problem, but the munching sounds were going to drive her out of her freaking gourd. And if she stopped the cookie flow, which she'd tried on several previous occasions, the narcoleptic slave demanded chips.

Then it started talking murder.

"Look, you're perfectly free to come out any time," said Dr. Flesh. "The coffin is unbolted. In fact, why don't you take a walk, get some fresh air, or make yourself useful. Have your cookies. Or get some more cookies.

"Here's some money"—she tossed a handful of bills towards the upright coffin. "But let me work in peace. Please. That's all I ask."

"You don't love me anymore," came the voice through a mouthful of cookie mush.

"Of course I love you," said Viola. "I am trying to concentrate on this ending. Where I wrap up the movie and ride into the sunset. Or we could put you in a sidecar like *Easy Rider.* Any helpful suggestions?"

"Gumballs," said Solare.

"Cookies, gumballs, murder, which is it?" said Viola. "We've discussed this. You can't just go out and randomly kill people."

"I can't?"

"No. I have to give you an order first. Then you specifically target certain people. People who have pissed me off or otherwise messed with my mix. I thought you were in a hypnotic trance?"

"It wore (munch, munch, chomp) off."

"Can't you just have a wank or something?"

"No porn."

"Oh, that's right. You demanded hermaphrodite porn or you were going to make my life a living hell, and devastate the earth for generations."

"I will be with you on your wedding night," said Solare.

"*It's been fucking done!*" said Dr. Flesh. "Get some original material."

Twas not always thus. They had met three years earlier, at the Hipster's Got a Brand New Sandwich Lotion Bar in Altendale. A transsexual, a hermaphrodite, an ironic mustache-shaped sandwich, and truly awful poetry to seal their affection.

"I stand here like railroad tracks," Solare had been drunkenly intoning from the stage, "and I'll kick your fucking ass if you don't applaud my poetry."

The reading had been going on for about three hours when Dr. Flesh walked in. There was something about an eight-foot gender-ambiguous thing in platform heels, glitter makeup and a rockabilly pompadour that was magic, especially when it was swaying back and forth and belting out bad Bukowski imitations.

Viola had been mesmerized by the sheer inverted genius of Solare's poems. They were so godawful they went beyond the realm of merely talentless drunken spew and briefly scraped the sublime. And retreated, and returned to spew, and resolved into a pathetic but oddly touching spectacle.

But that was years ago. Their period of domestic bliss had faded into a perpetual whine-fest. The thrill of sending Solare out to wreak terrible vengeance on her enemies had waned long ago. Only a small vestige of affection remained between them. Dr. Flesh kept to her work, and Solare sent out a lengthy litany of complaints from its coffin. The honeymoon was over, and the vibrations in the lab were increasingly fraught with overtones of homicide.

***

Tiffany Tiffany St. Tropez descended cautiously from the train, clutching the shoulder strap of her Gooshy Fruit bag. She was carrying a lot of bling today, and was afraid that some of it might wind up in the hands of terrorists.

What she couldn't figure out was what use the bling would serve them after they'd blown themselves up in a desperate act of Gee Hod. Maybe they'd give it to their virgin concubines? Whatever a concubine was.

Ms. St. Tropez was frequently bedeviled with questions of this nature. As an avid viewer of the Hot Fox News, she daily learned of developments that distressed her and made her stomach growl even more than usual.

Still, she was still hotter than most, and a steady intake of small salads was guaranteed to maintain the hotness. At least according to HFN.

The platform was deserted. She wondered what had happened to all the other passengers that got off with her. It was as if they'd been swallowed up.

Again, what-evs. Most of them were badly dressed and looked like they could stand an exclusively small salad diet themselves. And a few of them smelled bad.

Convinced finally that no Gee Hodist Satanic lesbians lurked in the shadows with pink umbrellas, she walked resolutely towards the Noe Street Exit. She tried to ignore the footsteps for as long as possible. Just deny it's happening, they said on the Hot Fox News. Pretend it's a movie. She took comfort in that advice until the eight-foot hermaphrodite in platform heels and glam rock makeup tapped her on the shoulder.

"What do you want?" she squealed, brandishing her pepper spray. "I've been trained, I know how to use this," she said, trying to recover her composure.

"You've got the spray pointed towards yourself," said the hermaphrodite in a deep, mellow voice. "Sorry, I didn't mean to scare you. I just thought I might interest you in a spectacle for the ages."

"Spectacles for the aged?" asked Tiffany. "Look, I already gave to charity last week, and I could barely afford this bag." She brandished the Gooshy Fruit in its face.

"That's a nice bag," said the hermaphrodite. "Very blingy. No, I said 'spectacle for the ages.' Would you like to see it?"

"As long as I don't have to like, rub shoulders with old people," said Tiffany primly. "Old people have diseases. It's a proven medical fact. I saw it on the HFN."

"I can assure you that the spectacle has very little to do with old people," said the hermaphrodite. "It's made for young, hot people like yourself. I have some tickets here for the show. Would you like one?"

Tiffany squinted at the proffered ticket. "Uh, I guess. Ok. As long as it's not horror. I hate horror."

The hermaphrodite was silent on this point.

"Is it funny?"

"Oh yes, very funny." Solare attempted a laugh.

"Okay, 'cause…I guess if it's free, and there aren't any gross old people, and it's not horror, and it's funny, I'll take a ticket."

The hermaphrodite gave her the ticket.

"Thanks," said Tiffany. But the creature had vanished.

Tiffany shook her head. "Weird!" she said to no one in particular. And stepped out onto the street.

***

Nathan Hale Bilge was not a happy camper. In fact, he hated that moronic phrase to begin with. So why had it automatically popped into his head? Bilge prided himself in his ability with the language, popping the bubble of cliché to make his critiques stylish and interesting, with fresh, happy phrases that exactly coincided with his meaning. Maybe he hadn't had enough sleep, or been hitting the Nyquil too hard—he also hated the term "abusing" when it applied to judicious use of over-the-counter medications for ends not intended by the manufacturer.

The entire setup reminded Bilge of that godawful book he'd eviscerated for all time on his blog. What was the title, *Blood Moon* or *Death 'Stroid*, something lame and moronic. As he recalled, it was a spin-off of a franchise he practically worshiped to distraction, and the author, Johansen, had actually made fun of his favorite monster character, Mason Borknees. Bilge had always secretly identified with the monster, who was kind of a Momma's boy who got kicked around a good deal and drowned when the camp counselors were off having a good time. When Mason took up the machete in the sequel to the original movie, Bilge had felt it down to his toes. Johansen had used all these words that he had either made up or taken straight from a thesaurus, because nobody actually *used* those words in a novel. Or anywhere.

Johansen was lucky to get two stars on Warrior.com. Especially from Bilge. He had a reputation to uphold, after all. So-called novelists who messed with continuity and made fun of Borknees deserved to be slowly dipped in sulfuric acid, starting with the toes. Worst of all, nobody had asked him, Nathan Hale Bilge, to write a book. Which was why he had to content himself with the blog.

***

The movie you are about to read conceives itself through you. You are the host and it is the organism. By turns, you may be expected to carry that weight.

In case of spontaneous ectoplasm, heat rash, dereliction of the body map or other extremes, orderlies are placed at the exits to assist. They have been designed in a superior lab by experts in Doom and thus cannot be taken except with an injection of the Dream Liquid straight to the retina.

Dr. Flesh is a luminous being who shapes her contours from your dreams. She stands at the top of a ladder placing huge letters into slots on the Marquee de Sade. She is wearing your favorite fetish gear.

From now on you will be free to design her, provided she has access to all of your files and their Lords.

III.

Viola had spent hours and hours in the warehouse laboratory to no effect. The attempt to create a Dream Liquid—a medium by which the minds of her audience would partake of, recreate and alter the movie from within—had so far proved futile. She felt like a mutant, postmodern Edison, her lab table cluttered with filaments and soaked with 90% perspiration.

Fucking Edison. She hated that guy, yet trial and error had produced a few rare, if useless, triumphs. Gerbil Man still cycled endlessly; the Self-Serve apparatus for auto-cannibalism had been a surprising hit with the local German community. And Fart Box worked even better than expected, enhanced with Reichian orgones—a tonic blast of pure flatulence always changed one's perspective.

Until she arrived at a solution—quite literally.

Impatient with bodily functions, Viola had taken to peeing in a bucket rather than leaving the lab to heed the call of nature. Tired, her overtaxed mind teeming with artfully constructed neon squiggles, she once accidentally squatted over a beaker instead.

The beaker was prepped with radiated recombinant DNA from a wolverine in heat. So far, the DNA had not adhered to the salamander genes or the tight Levi's 501's. Until now.

As she hastily rose from the squatting position, impatient lest she miss a single second of the process, she observed the love match of the pee, the wolverine cells and the genetic material she'd cloned from the dream-state of celebrities and tossed together in a loving salad.

The pee molecules bound themselves in loving harmony with the others; the solution glowed bright yellow. Then the liquid began to circulate through the pipes, resolving in a thick, steady drip from the nozzle hooked over the basin at the end of the long steel workbench.

It looked and acted like Dream Liquid. All that was missing was a test subject.

"Solare," she yelled, "I've got something for you."

"Yes Mistress?"

"Remember Mistress's attempts to create a medium for the Reality Stack?"

"Yes Mistress," said Solare, recalling with supreme horror the many tortures it had experienced as a beta tester for Dr. Flesh. The rack, the screws, the vibrating pumpkin, an exceedingly hollow feeling in the guts, and the replacement of that hollow feeling with a painful fullness.

***

She was a long way from home—Oklahoma, the "Okay State," where concepts like genderfuck and forced feminization barely registered. Like a comforting mother, the Church and its doctrines had always been there, relieving her doubts and answering her anxious questions with simple, unqualified dogma: Life begins at conception. Birth control is frowned upon. Never question the priest, even when he pulls down your underwear and puts something hard and painful back there.

Viola had been born into a world on fire, a time of change and unrest. Back in the Summer of '69, Oklahoma City first discovered hippies, free love and the fresh, disturbing notion that women and other minorities might not be as happy with second-class citizenship as formerly anticipated.

The social and cultural changes were matched by changes in the urban landscape. When Viola was born, the Crosstown Expressway had just been built for I-40, which only went as far as El Reno. At Oklahoma State, minor tear gas was expressed and a few long-haired students carried signs around the cafeteria in protest of Vietnam.

Fortunately for the greater good, the bane of drug use was limited to squalid quarters where lonely hipsters, alienated from good society for experimenting with mind-bending loco weed, tried to cultivate a taste for cocktails.

Despite these developments, however, certain things remained the same. Things that would never be okay in the Okay State.

Being gay was one of them. Using multisyllabic words was another. And never, under any circumstances, was a sex change permissible. Such a concept revolted against God, Christ, the Creator's law.

At 13, Viola—then Bob Simpson—had a revelation. Bob had begged to be excused from church due to a violent, hacking cough, and his parents had begrudgingly accepted his absence from Sunday services. As soon as he heard the station wagon pull out of the driveway, Bob rolled out of bed, already fully dressed, and walked next door to where his neighbors were having a garage sale.

These neighbors had never been popular, and after a few months of trying to make peace with the stolid citizens of Nichols Hills, the young couple had finally decided to pack their bags and go west.

Bob had always liked the couple. They were young, well-spoken, educated and, most important, accepted him the way he was. On the few occasions he'd spent time with them, when his parents were off doing church-related social activities, the Corsos made Bob feel welcome, inviting him into their house to listen to music, talk about art, politics, science and philosophy. They were passionate about ideas, about changing the world. Nobody else in

Bob's life had the slightest interest in changing anything, except maybe the wallpaper.

He couldn't believe they were letting go of all these books, magazines and records for a handful of change. But moving was expensive, and the Corsos needed whatever cash they could scrape together. Which meant leaving behind such treasures as *Alladin Sane* by David Bowie, a complete chemistry set, books on anatomy, physiology and general biology, and five years' worth of *Rolling Stone* and *Famous Monsters*.

Stowing these finds away in his closet and under his bed underneath the more socially acceptable baseball equipment, Bob conceived a plan. He would follow the Corsos west, taste the worlds that beckoned from the pages of the books and magazines, that called to him from the grooves of the Bowie record.

At 17, after saving up some money from odd jobs, Bob took a Greyhound. Away from constrictions, away from prejudice, away from small minds and dogma, to the big, bad West Coast, where entire neighborhoods, whole cities, were devoted to acts that filled him with mingled desire and horror. Sodom and Gomorrah was his new home.

After Sweden and the sex change, Bob had his name legally changed to Viola Flesh, the new moniker arising spontaneously from a marathon showing of Andy Warhol movies and the erotic nightmares that beset him afterwards. Medical school and film school followed swiftly. Then came the bizarre synthesis, the experiments, the rerouting of synaptic connections in the service of new appetites.

What drove Viola, had driven her since she was a boy in Oklahoma City, was a will to transgression. The very idea of givens, universal laws, infuriated her. She had wrestled with the thorniest challenges of philosophy and theology, grappled head-on with such matters as the existence of good and evil, the possibility of a universe driven by pure chance, the conditions under which life became possible, and further—the nature of life itself, and its relationship to unlife (she hated the idea of death, it seemed to her prosaic and lacking in imagination). She had a Faustian heart, but without the old alchemist's weakness and vacillation.

Viola was unimpressed by limits. Even the greatest thinkers admitted a point where knowledge was impossible. That, to Viola, lessened their stature. Moderation, conservatism, such values she suspected to be concessions, and thus flawed. If there was a point to it all, she wanted to know. If there was no point, she wanted to know. But more and more she suspected that the posing of limits derived from fear, whether of social opprobrium or a starker, metaphysical terror: madness and its hinterlands.

Dr. Flesh was comfortable with madness, in love with horror, and thus, at least within herself, had come to terms with ideas considered diabolic, sick, evil and wrong to most of the human bacteria crawling the planet. They were stuck with a fundamental defect of reasoning; in Western logical structure, things were either one way or the complete opposite. Dialectics informed the limits of the possible. Things were either true or false, right or wrong. Hybridity, fluidity, the leaking of substance from one conceptual category to another, was disallowed.

**

At first, she believed that the pain, intolerance and prejudice she encountered was part of the not-her. With all her might, she built a barrier between Her and Them. Even as Bob Simpson, she had thought of it that way: a personal Berlin Wall.

But silently, secretly and inexorably, the not-her had found a way in. Worming through the chinks in her psyche. Testing fissures, weak areas, points of entry. And slowly, inevitably, the not-her set up shop in her soul, and started making demands.

Kill for me, it said.

Destroy.

The not-her had power, composed of the internalized hate, envy, jealousy and projection of all the others. It was a monster. An impossibly idealized form, what they themselves could not achieve, a monster of sex and allure, with wolverine claws and a studied, sculpted smile.

It was perfectly hideous. But it was perfect.

Viola Flesh was the first complete and successful creation of Dr. Flesh. Who, working through Bob's body, tore out the human heart and replaced it with an exact duplicate, cold, efficient and deadly. This duplicate heart would never again hammer hotly at insult. It would not experience the pain, merely process it and send it directly to the command and control center.

A metal heart that could never die.

As they had not recognized or nurtured his gentleness and openness, She was sealed to their humanity as well.

As they had spurned him, she would make them suffer. Endlessly.

The Bilges of the world, their impotent rage at the truly talented transformed into web-based vomit. The cutesy, ever-so-normal girls so nice they named her twice. Tiffany Tiffany St. Lopez. Or Brittany—god she adored it—Brittany Lapierre. These guinea pigs were chosen by a piece of software Flesh had built herself, a heat-seeking missile for plastic girls and cardboard men.

Such as Matt Gooch, the Death Ball hero of Sugar Valley High, with his rippling abs, his sneer of deprecation for anybody who didn't fit his narrow standards, his steroid-induced ferocity belied by a coward's heart. The man with the pee stream for non-blonds, golden showers for golden girls, and steaming piss for blood.

Dr. Flesh is unaware who made who. Ultimately, the not-her has replaced her. Cell by cell. Molecule by molecule. Unwittingly, she has collaborated with her deadliest enemies. Unknowingly, she has become the thing she hates.

IV.

In all of Sugar Valley, one school dominated.

J. Edgar Reagan High, known familiarly as Sugar Valley High, was the cynosure of all eyes. Its scholars went to the Ivy Leagues in packed limousines, its athletes waded in gore, its young women were prized for their beauty, taste in fashion and fastidious diets, and its nerds were tolerated for the prestige they brought the school—but just barely.

The most dominant in a heavy-hitting pack, Matt Gooch littered the Death Ball field with bloody corpses, his trademark 'Berzerker cry' carried to the top of the bleachers and echoed by his many fans.

His entire being itched with the need to twist the nerd's head around until it almost snapped, smear him with his own dribbled feces and make him perform oral in a non-gay way, when someone tapped him on the shoulder.

"Oh, Mr. Kriege, I was just helping this poor, unfortunate scholar. Someone must have attacked him and perpetrated terrible acts on his person. I hate to see that happen."

But it wasn't Mr. Kriege. It was an eight-foot hermaphrodite with a hellbilly pompadour.

"Huh?"

Solare thrust two tickets into his hands and strode off.

Gooch examined the tickets, muttering "what the fuck?" They were yellow, 3" by 4," with a picture of some kind of monster superimposed on a metallic background. The monster's eye-holes were punched through. In very small letters at the bottom read "Reality Stack, One Night Only. No passes or substitutions."

He was about the throw it away when he remembered what the blog had said. Psychogremlin.com was a must-read for Gooch and his pack. Always a kick to read what the nerds had to say about their weird-ass obsessions.

Had Bilge known that his most avid readers consisted of a group of beef-pumped jocks who would probably kick his ass on sight, chances are he would opt for another vocation. But as often he opined in his multisyllabic, snarky way on whatever fanboy product came down the pike, Gooch and his pack gathered in garages over beer kegs and ridiculed his pronouncements. Half the time they didn't understood what the freak he was going on about, which was half the fun of reading him. Supernerd Bilge had devoted his last column to this new movie, known only as "Reality Stack," which was being sneak-previewed to a randomly-chosen audience.

There were two tickets, so he could invite someone. A girl. Obviously, because he wasn't a queer, and only took it in the ass once, purely by accident, in the showers. Gooch prided himself on his heterosexuality. He'd fucked 85% of the female population of the school, the remainder being those considered Not So Hot. Essentially, he was a stud. A guy's guy.

"This ticket's for Brittany," he decided immediately. Yes, definitely. The rush he got from thinking about Brittany was so intense that he forgot all about the nerd, who had stopped breathing anyway. Let the groundskeeper find him, thought Gooch. Didn't Spanish people love twisted corpses anyway?

The date Gooch had set his sights on was one of five Brittany's registered at Sugar Valley High, but the only one he hadn't plowed with his 12-inch wood. Brittany Lapierre and

Tiffany Tiffany St. Tropez vied for the title of Hottest Babe at Sugar Valley, but Lapierre was considered slightly hotter because of her ass tattoo. Which also marked her as Sluttiest Ho at Sugar Valley. Not necessarily a bad thing, as long as you were blonde.

He could just see it: Gooch, Lapierre, a darkened screening room, his hand on her thigh, her purring, his hand creeping up her skirt, her little cry of surprise, his fingers plucking the elastic of her panties, seeking and stroking her shaved vajay, as some nerd shit played on the screen. As far as he knew, Lapierre wasn't exactly a fangirl, and knew as much about art cinema as the groundskeeper, Lopez. Which couldn't be much.

"Oh my gosh," gushed Brittany. "Really? You thought of me? I don't know, I have to check my calendar. Hold on one teensy little sec, ok? Here we go. I have an app for appointments, all I have to do is text myself and it works it all out for me, and then I get a special ring tone an hour before. What's it called? What day? Reality Snack—that sounds lame. But whatever. You say it's good? What's it about?"

Gooch maintained his masculine silence as Brittany babbled to herself for another ten minutes. "Ok," she said finally, looking up. "I can do it. Pick me up at 7:00?"

"Sure thing," said Gooch.

"Yes," he whooped as soon as he was out of earshot. "I am so going to score. Thanks for the tickets, Assface."

***

"Where the hell are we?"

"I don't know," said Gooch. "Looks like a rough neighborhood. But don't worry, babe. I can protect you."

"Wha…?" asked Brittany. "Sorry, I've gotta take this. Hello? Yeah, Wonder Boy has driven us off the map. It's all like gross and sketchy here. And I could swear I just saw a homeless—no, wait, it's just some old clothes. But whatever."

Gooch had to admit they were far from home. These were not the manicured lawns of Sugar Valley. There were a lot of tattered and graffiti-tagged billboards for an off brand of malt liquor. And though he wasn't positive, and no way he was telling Brittany, he was pretty sure he just saw the old clothes scratch themselves as they shuffled down the boulevard.

"Don't you have like a GPS on this thing?" she asked, making a face. "And I can't get bars on this piece of crap." She shook her cell phone, but it was just going crazy on her. She put it up to her ear again. "Hello? Crap! I should have stayed home and read *500 Shades of Man Gravy*. It was getting really good. Dorian had these, like, special balls you put in your vajay…"

"It's gonna be okay," said Gooch, who wished to Bob he'd never seen that he/she/it with the weirdo tickets, had trusted his guts and told the eight-foot-tall boygirl to fuck the fuck off. And he was missing his favorite show, *The Karpathians*. Muffy Karpathian was pregnant by the Fresh Prince of Darkness and she was about to give birth to the Spawn, and Missy was getting her nails done.

"I guess as long as we're here, we might as well make the best of it," said Brittany primly. She had learned this deep philosophy from the Hot Fox News. "Right? You agree with me. Right?"

"Sure, Brittany," said Gooch, wishing he had asked Tiffany Tiffany instead. Who, granted, didn't have the ass tattoo, but he had a feeling he was going to see that tonight anyway. He wished he was home watching that new 3D Just Quim Beaver video, the one where he took off his pants. Slowly. If you slowed it down frame by frame, you could see Beaver's cock.

***

Viola slips her gloved hand into the murk at the bottom of the tank and her body is bathed in the violet light from clusters of bulbs that line the top and sides. The leathery sacs are squirming at the bottom and about to deliver their payload. They resemble fried eggs, or, alternatively, eyeballs. From the pupil-like center a squirt of jet black ink emerges as from a squid. The squirts of ink form tiny balls the size and consistency of the tapioca balls in Japanese novelty drinks. She pulls a handful of the balls—seeds—out of the tank, opens up a chute behind the hulking mass of the bio-digital conversion machine and carefully places them in a row, then slams the chute home. In 24 hours the seeds will hatch into characters to populate the Reality Stack.

V.

Dr. Flesh dreams herself into the narrative.

Her essence, evaporated and streamed into a play of photons, charges the screen from one of the Camjector lenses. It is then scooped up, remixed and mingled with the dreams, hopes and fears of the audience. Below the twin lenses lies a jagged mouth, the entry point for chaos.

The mouth belches forth lies and mystifications.

The Eyeball Bondage set adheres to the one who wears it. It, like the Camjector and its film, is a live thing. At first one dons the set like a pair of 3D glasses and prepares for the usual thrill ride. But the EB set meanwhile does a retinal scan, then a brain scan, dividing the cerebral cortex into slices that it copies and twists. A mindfuck in multiple dimensions.

Like the clockwork god of the Deists, Dr. Flesh sets a universe in motion; unlike that god, she is present always in multiple forms, but powerless to change the outcome. She has placed a replica of herself within the movie itself, directing the movie from within. But the audience has also been gifted with the powers of the auteur. At any point the narrative may switch tracks. At any terminus in the tracks, rogue ganglia may upset the stage and deliver the outcome.

Axons become axes, synapses fuse and dissolve into golden idols. The movie hacks itself, now dominant, now submissive. The audience is diffused, eyeballs slipped through eyeshooks as minds shrink to primitive lenses.

Concussive blow of a new splatter metaphysics.

The mouth yawns: jagged teeth crunch the props cum scenery cum audience cum narrative. There are no governors as the biofilm is edited from within and without, protease clippers moving with the precision of a factory of amok fleshbots. Now we see that the landscape has been poured and the scenarios prepped, as Flesh's beta crew, her test bunnies, take their places.

And deliver their lines.

A storm of lights pour off the Marquee De Sade and genuflect at her feet, batting away her protests. "It's all for you," say the lights. "It's all for you, this magnificent dream, these radiating signals, these patterns of murder, this orifice of sucking energy, the parade of pink shells undulating down the streets of dream."

The audience leans in and sees that she is made of billions and billions of tiny stories. Each story generates another, which is the seed of an entirely fresh creation. As she reads, the audience will reformat spontaneously. Goons are placed at all exits with orders to shoot heretics on sight with magic foaming bullets.

Dr. Flesh clears her throat and gulps from the manuscript. She complains that the light hurts her eyes. She drinks a glass of water which is full of eyeballs. She spears one of the eyeballs with a toothpick and places it between her pretty lips.

There is rapt silence. She pops the eyeball like a cherry tomato and thanks you for your patience.

"The text you are about to see has no precedent and spontaneously recreates itself in your image. Criticism based on a stable and not fluctuating narrative—at least insofar as the narrative does not change based on your biostreams, lights, dashes, colors and wandering virus—is an ancient remedy to an old disease. The ways of our ancestors were largely ponderous and stuck in ruts. We suggest that you jettison now any preconceived ideas about what a narrative is, should be, could be or might be. This film is impossible to analyze as it ripples through your mind like a prism and throws off new, spontaneous narrative like shrugged viral seeds. Any attempt to become the host will result in becoming the parasite your mothers warned you about. And as we all know, that ain't a pretty sight for sore eyes."

She paused to laugh at her own cryptic joke. A large man in a rumpled Lakers T-shirt made for one of the exits but was taken down by Syd Field's screenplay formula and a phalanx of Joseph Campbell clones wearing the masks of Greek tragedy.

"Orderlies are positioned at all X/Y coordinate points of the theater in case of green goo, lightning strikes, Lovecraftian incursions, Phil K. Dickian revelations or the sudden manifestation of three-eyed crablike creatures from non-Euclidean spacetime. This theater may contain multiple manifolds with protease enzymes carefully calibrated to digest you like a vitamin pill. Spontaneous body melts are not uncommon.

"Once the film passes the projector head it is automatically knit with your thoughts, emotions, feelings, power, powerlessness, wretchedness and sense of doom and/or immortality and/or immorality. Fashion sense is not an option, although if you wait in the lobby area some will be provided to you in return for your skin and another, random tissue sample.

"The movie has been so designed with engines of loving craft that as you watch it, you will be helplessly sucked into a powerful story of two lovers, light-beings from beyond the parameters of this universe, who occasionally manifest as toys, fishlights, reptiles, green goo and the monolithic dome. Also as unmotivated bodies from which the liquid has been drained spontaneous. All X/Y coordinate points of the theater have been swabbed for your protection. Small children may suddenly emerge as robotic savants and hit the ground ruining. Architects of the abyss are standing by with peyote rays and machineguns that shoot viral vision. There will be Christmas on Earth. I now present the fabulous opera."

The audience adjusts Eyeball Bondage headgear that came of age in Samoa. The headgear inserts a hypodermic needle directly into the retina and replaces eyeball fluid with the Dream Liquid. Once the Dream Liquid has circulated through all micropores, the audience is instant jelly and amenable to the darkest of propaganda. Although Dr. Flesh is not a sadist, she exults in this precise moment, as the audience has self-selected, itself a guinea pig, the genuine article. Masochists have special attachments to their genitalia that lance them with prismatic splatter should they project too much.

She carefully threads the biofilm into the projector, a Cyclopean mass of green moss-choked headstone from Easter Island graves. The projector masticates the biofilm and sweats furiously, little oily droplets trickling down and forming a river between the aisles.

The EB headgear allows the audience to see the islands in this river as they fluctuate and pop in and out of focus. Dr. Flesh may now directly interact with the unconscious. She watches as the biofilm squirts its toxic byproducts into the rivers which have become choked with leaves and bits of brainstem.

VI.

Gooch had seen virgin beaches like this in the movies, but now he was in one. For real.

He dipped his hand in the wet sand and brushed it on his cheek. "That freaky doctor chick was right," he said. "We are so there." Since it was only a movie, he was pretty sure he could fuck both of the girls. They'd have to let him. And there were no worries about getting pregnant, because the freaky doctor chick said it was…he hadn't exactly tracked what she said. And then they'd had to sign that form, which he hadn't exactly tracked either, although he'd caught something about the chance of sudden death and had to fill in the names of his next of kin.

But Gooch was not one to dwell on the negatives. No, as an avid fan of Dr. Grue Ponsky on the Hot Fox, he knew that the way to health, wealth and hot ass was to always see the sunny side of things. "Keep looking towards the sun," Dr. Grue would remind his viewers. Gooch was pretty sure he didn't mean that literally.

"So how about that three-way?" he asked. Getting no reply, he turned around.

He was completely alone on the beach. No girls, no three-way, just miles and miles of white sand.

***

Bilge wonders if he should take a break, set down the headset and maybe get some popcorn. He can't remember whether there was a concession stand, and the entrance to the screening room itself shuffles in his mind like a deck of cards. At first he was standing before a flight of stairs that he presumed led directly into the room, and could hear what sounded like previews for upcoming productions.

He has already confirmed in his own mind the terrible review he will give the movie, assured that his pronouncements on the thing will curdle any appetite to fork out hard-earned cash to see the bloody thing.

"Another Grim Enigma from the Mind of Dr. Flesh" is the title he has settled on.

But the headset is nowhere to be found. And neither is the theater.

Bilge is somewhat impressed. However flawed Flesh's concepts, however bewildering and overly complicated her storylines, she—or an army of molecular biologists—have truly delivered on the promise of a new film technology. If only someone else held the reins. Someone like Bilge himself, perhaps.

Bilge had originally wanted to become a filmmaker himself, but none of his projects got off the ground. He suspected that they were too radical, because too much smacking of original genius, for the dull-brained titans that controlled the purse strings of Hollyweird. Nobody wanted new anymore; they wanted proven, they wanted nostalgia tweaked slightly for a new generation. They wanted asses in seats and sealed mouths, they wanted an audience whipped through a tunnel of sinister wonders and rendered like sausage, just as the movies were links packed with the meat derived from other movies, ad nauseum sayeth the Lard.

Which is why, instead of standing at the helm of his own project, his own Reality Stack—which he would never title Reality Stack, that was stupid—he was preparing to grind out a formulaic response to a movie he did not intend to watch all the way through. If he could just find his way out of the movie.

Flesh had said something in her introduction about exits that fluctuated with the audience's perceived capacity for suffering, whatever the fuck that meant. Bilge felt he had already suffered plenty, and thus had proved himself worthy of an exit, a quick escape to the parking lot, a hop on the freeway and a return to his bachelor quarters, the Mac stack, the spank mags, the popcorn and the power seat.

But that fucking Thing had taken him off the power seat and made him one of her lab subjects. Worst of all, he had stepped right into it.

There had to be some clue to the exits. He scanned the sky, which blinked back at him, a calm blue suffused with the subtle lineaments of his own eye sockets, his own retina. He was staring back at himself staring back at himself with the blinking cursor light at the edge of the retinal scan sprouting a question mark. Where exits?

This was not an exit. This was not an entrance. This was a dream of drowning.

But his hands were the same. His feet were the same. If he could find a mirror, Bilge was pretty sure his face would be the same as well. His nicely manicured goatee, the black-rimmed glasses, the trendy shaved head. And, admittedly, the paunch that rose beneath; but he'd always been big-boned, and he loved those potato chips.

❋❋❋

Okay, first of all, this was not her idea of a good time. She was a special girl with special needs—wait, that made her sound like a fucktard. Where was the reset symbol when you needed to click on it?

Tiffany Tiffany prided herself on having a clue, and for once in her life, she was clueless. Her environment had sorted itself out around her, and rather than it being a product of her—like in that movie with Jack Nicholson—she was a product of it. Regardless, if she'd known she was going to have to act in a movie she would have passed on the ticket. This was bullshit. Her hair was all wrong, her clothes were all wrong, she would need to lose at least 30 pounds and maybe just get a complete makeover plus a layer of synthetic skin.

It was too late to binge and purge. Was she on camera now? How could you be inside a movie anyway? She wished she had paid attention to what the domme-dyke had said about, what was it, biofilm, and how the movie was a living organism that changed according to the mind of the viewer, their deepest wishes and fears…not that she minded complicated, but this was nerd-complicated, and if she wanted to stress over something dense, she would rather it be not boring, and lame. All of which this movie idea was, and then some.

But it was too late now.

What if the movie turned her into a lesbian? Or worse—one of those chicks with dicks? What if she gained weight, not like a small salad that didn't really add anything, but actual weight…and she couldn't find a toilet? Would she have to blow chunks in the street? In this filthy, disgusting, unpaved street, where—she shuddered—homeless non-blonds and un-Americans were free to wander around at will? What if she encountered foreigners? Or terrorists? Or Europeans—and not the awesome couture kind, but people—she guessed you had to call them that, because you couldn't shoot them, much—people of, what was the term, difference?

And her cell was not working. She couldn't get bars. She couldn't click her heels and say "There's no place like home," because she wasn't wearing heels. And even if she were, they wouldn't work with the dirt road and the tarpaper shacks and the weed smokers…she could distinctly smell that hateful substance. Stoners were just so gross. And completely rude.

***

Dr. Flesh slipped down through the soft meat of the darkfield until she hit the jungle floor. It was then that she spotted them.

Doppelgangers.

A few were hiding behind the thick leaves of the enormous trees that rose until they shut out the sky. Others stirred her peripheral vision like soup.

"Oh hell no," she said. And then she remembered Solare's warning when she began to incubate the eggs in the medium of her own cloned brain tissue. "Some of those things are gonna become little tiny Viola Fleshes." For a mindless slave, Solare had flashes of insight that shocked and scared her at times. Where did she pick up these tidbits of information? As it happened, Solare was right—again.

When she moved, they moved. When she reached for her cinegun, they did likewise. The cinegun spat its charge. And Tiffany Tiffany toppled from her perch and tumbled to the ground. Dr. Flesh heard the doubles chattering. The things they were saying about her were not pleasant. An echo chamber of her doubts and insecurities redoubled unto infinity.

Her only hope to thwart the doubles lay in the narrative flux governor she had built into the darkfield early in the production of the Reality Stack. But that meant introducing an element of sheer chaos into the story stream. Suddenly, she heard movement behind her. A watery, slushy noise. She squatted quickly down as the semen jet splashed over Tiffany Tiffany's prone body, webbing it in goo.

This did not belong to the plan either.

***

"Your Jello is ready, Mistress," said Solare.

"Silence, Worm," responded Dr. Flesh.

"Please stop saying that," pleaded Solare. "One of these days you're really going to hurt my feelings."

"And the problem with that scenario would be…" Dr. Flesh let the question resonate in the stillness of the lab.

Solare smiled thoughtfully. "I'd rather you hurt my body," it said.

"I know, but hurt feelings last longer."

The Jello had been hard-won. She had at last decided upon cherry as the appropriate flavor for Tiffany Tiffany's clit-mold, considering how she had plucked so many fresh sufferings from the girl. It was probably hard for her to even conceive, in the Whitey White suburban bastion of Sugar Valley, how many things could go wrong for a blonde.

Like losing her pussy to an insane transsexual film director slash medical deviant. At first, Dr. Flesh had attempted to cultivate the clit-mold without damaging the guinea pig, but the girl's excessive wriggling, screaming and bad attitude had made that approach impossible. It was all her fault, after all, that the mold couldn't be obtained without bodily harm. First of all, said the Hypocritical Oath, do much harm. Or was it, do harm until the concept of harm itself became a permeable membrane through which an entire battalion of harms could be gleefully shoved? But that was theory. The praxis was another thing.

And sometimes praxis got sloppy. Dr. Flesh thought of Louis Pasteur and his filthy lab. Without slop, there would be no antibiotics. Without pain, there could be no pleasure. Without removing the entire vajay, there could be no cherry-flavored clit Jello.

She plucked one at leisure from the tray. A little sprinkling of angel dust made the Jello so much more than it already was, a model for the sheer mutability of matter. What had Heraclitus said about not stepping in the same river twice? With just a soupcon of PCP, every clit-mold became its own universe, a chance to disappear briefly from the scene.

She was happy to have conceived the notion of directing the movie from inside. As the biofilm was a more or less literal simulacrum of her desire, every guinea pig whose consciousness informed the Reality Stack would also become a director. In essence, there were many movies jostling to be made within a loose organic structure that was itself alive.

The whitey white girl's clit—and the vajay—floated in sterile solution in the main fridge. Casually popping another cherry-flavored cosmos of hallucinogenic flavor, Dr. Flesh eased open the fridge door and examined the pussy itself. Aside from ragged cuts at the edges, unavoidable considering the guinea pig's refusal to stay still, it was a piece of perfection. She strapped on sterile gloves, reached into the fridge and placed the pussy on the operating table.

Marvelous. A true work of art.

She reached into the jar, pulled out the organ and placed it in the collagen base. She thumbed it, spread it open and inhaled deeply. For a girl with such an ugly spirit, she had a remarkably savory vajay.

She pondered the question of eating it raw, or cooking it. Yes, she would definitely cook it, slow-simmered in its own juices, and garnished with its own cherry-flavored clit, reproduced endlessly around the borders.

Maybe she would serve it to the girl, make her eat it. Eat her own pussy. That was a thought.

These questions made her moist. Such conundrums, such complex reflections, such sweet Epicurean agony.

She clicked on the monitor in the girl's room, wondering how she was holding up after the cauterization.

Not well, evidently. Tiffany Tiffany was banging about the walls of the padded cell, screaming about giant spiders. Had she gone completely sideways? Then Viola remembered about the infusions, the drug cocktails. Ah yes, whitey-white girl would be suffering from horrible hallucinations right about now.

"Let's tune in and watch," murmured the Directress to herself. It had been relatively easy to plug the biosoft vector directly into the girl's brain, so she could watch the progress of her molting reality.

VII.

Where in the name of fuck was she? Back in her bedroom at last, it would appear, the comforting all-pink Princess theme décor, her posters of boy bands, the sketch of the ass-tat she wanted so badly, that would make her exactly the same as that Brittany bitch. No, better, because Brittany's ass-tat read "For Daddy Only" and that was just gross. Tiffany Tiffany hoped she had better taste.

She turned on the lamp next to her bed, which worked; she clicked it on and off again several times just to be sure. Upstairs she could hear her mom and one of her many rich, handsome boyfriends going at it, which struck just the right note of realism but made her gorge rise and not in the good, thinning way. Plaster flakes drifted from the ceiling like the "dried maggot skin" episode of the Carpathians or that awful story her grandmother told the 9th Grade campers about "Necro Fanny." Her mom sounded like a hyena being sodomized with a jackhammer. It was so wrong. But at least it was home.

She frantically sought her iPod, which was right where she'd left it, and thumbed the volume just in time to catch the first chords of the new Baylor Twit song, which expressed everything Tiffany Tiffany desired in her life: a hot guy to buy her stuff, and how amazing she would look at the Senior Prom, and how he would marry her but leave her alone too so she could explore her options. She'd read an article in *Cosmology* on exactly that subject: "You're Mega-hot, so Why Settle For Just One Guy?"

To which Tiffany Tiffany had responded "exactly," and underscored many of the paragraphs with yellow HiLiter. The non-so-hot, the slightly-less-hot and the butt-reekingly gross would just have to rely on their personalities or whatever. She had something better than that. Her body.

Just to be sure that nothing funny had happened to that prized commodity in the interim, she decided to check herself out in the full-length mirror next to the closet.

At first she couldn't believe what she was seeing, then she believed, and then she understood, and then she wept. She had hoped it was all a dream—the hermaphrothingy thing, the yellow ticket, the skuzzy theater, the skanky dyke-hag saying all those things that made no sense, and then winding up on this unpaved dirt road surrounded by non-blonds who were *checking her out—* as if—listening to that ganga stoner music and surrounding her like some kind of wolf pack.

Then there was a sudden piercing sensation between her shoulderblades, dreams thick with the smell of bleach, waking up bound, gagged and being transported through a jungle, slung upside down from a pole, while the same non-blond dudes a weird song that was definitely not "Hakuna Matata" and she was pretty sure translated into "Gang-fuck the white bitch." They were the kind to do it, too.

***

Next to the mirror stood another mirror, and this mirror had a mate, and on and on, until Tiffany Tiffany found herself in a vast hall of mirrors, each of which depicted her in a slightly different way.

Just in case this was a dream and she really would wake up, she pinched herself. "Ow," she said, her fingers sinking right to the bone. That was a good thing, right—zero percent body fat? So why did she look like a raggedy ass skeleton bitch who'd been subsisting on small salads for most of her pretty hot life?

Her skeletal reflection grinned, and Tiffany Tiffany wept with horror.

To the immediate right of this mirror, she beheld another image, the exact opposite, which was straight out of that *Cosmology* article titled "Why Nobody Loves Your Fat Ass: 10 Easy Steps to Starvation." The "before" picture.

Tiffany screamed.

And screamed.

The images screamed back. The skeleton bitch did that face like that painting she'd never quite understood, with that howling guy on the bridge and the weird, ugly color scheme. The "before" picture shot her the finger.

The third image was a relief. In this reflection, she was back to her usual self, the one she'd modeled on the article "How to Tease Boys into Getting You Stuff." The tweaked eyebrows, the wide-eyed, virginal stare, straight into the camera; the mild pout with big swelling raspberry pouty lips, with her hands modestly placed over her naughty parts.

Yes, thought Tiffany Tiffany, it *had* been a dream, or a nightmare, before. This was the real her. The one who only put out for Daddy.

No, wait, that wasn't her at all. That was Brittany. It was in fact a reflection of her nemesis, the detested ass-tat girl.

She stamped her pretty little foot, which usually summoned a whole horde of buffed-out guys. But nobody came. It was too late to do anything about it, but Tiffany Tiffany was sure of one thing: if she ever got out of this lame movie, and talked to her daddy, who would talk to his high-powered attorney, the bitch would regret every last second of the day she was born, and probably other stuff too.

Being suspended upside down in a cage while brutal non-blonds poked at her with sharpened sticks was not her idea of a good time. And not only had Dr. Flesh denied her the small salads that sustained her, she had laid out a hideous spread thick with carbs. Tiffany Tiffany choked down the image and pushed it deep into her subconscious mind. Never, never again would she take the small salads for granted. But first there was the matter of denial.

Find your happy place, her counselor had told her. So what was her happy place? It certainly did not involve being forced to deep-throat a spiked strap-on dildo till her lips were raggedy clumps of flesh. Among other things the bitch would pay for, Tiffany Tiffany's extensive reconstructive cosmetic plastic surgery stood at the very top of the list. Maybe this was a good thing, then, because according to the Hot Fox, there was no such thing as being too hot, looking too good, or having enough authentic bling.

Tiffany Tiffany tried to smile, but she couldn't feel her face. Could that be her happy place, then—all eyes upon her as she strode to the stage, modestly denying all the compliments thrown her way, as she accepted the trophy for, what, best-looking, most blonde, blingiest?

It wasn't easy using her own mind to think of stuff. She usually relied on the Hot Fox for that, or her smart but not-so-hot friends, or her counselor at Sugar Valley High. She didn't like to admit she saw a counselor, because that made her a girl with problems, like those wretched creeps with bad hair and skin who hung out at the Drama Club talking about, she didn't know what, but it was lame. But her counselor usually told her things that made sense.

And what was that horrible music? Dr. Flesh must be operating again. No, no, don't think of that. Think of something happy and nice. With sugar on top. No, no sugar, that turned into fat, and fat turned into something she didn't even want to think about. Being unpopular.

And somebody was poking her with a sharp stick—again!

***

"DRUGS! I MUST HAVE DRUGS!" screamed Dr. Flesh.

Dragging one foot behind itself, Solare lurched into the operating room. "Lives, lives for the mawstah," it droned in a thick cockney accent.

"SOLARE! THE NEEDLE!"

"You might want to take off the caps lock," said Solare.

"SILENCE, WORM! I MADE YOU, AND I CAN UNMAKE YOU."

"True," said Solare. Viola had an excellent point. The makings and the unmakings had been several, many of them truly barbaric and nasty. At one point Solare had sported three cocks, one springing from its forehead. Dr. Flesh had used it roughly before throwing it away wet, and Solare had to comfort itself with a *Karpathians* marathon, Chunky Monkey and Kleenex. It could still feel the slime that clung to its body after the session. Fortunately, Dr. Flesh had relented, excised the second and third cock and turned the first one inside out, which was easier on

Solare. It liked having a pussy. It disliked being a thing. It wanted to have a normal life.

VIII.

Gooch could swear he recognized some of the faces on the masks: Columbus Lincoln, for example, who had liberated the indigenous people of the Americas from their reliance on natural resources and given them useful jobs involving gardening shears and leafblowers. He swelled up with blond pride just to think of his forebear's great legacy.

And then there was, of course, Reagan Hoover, who prosecuted the secret war against the commie gorillas in the jungles of San Nicaragua, and peacefully brought an end to the sufferings of the good Christian people of that country, who only wanted to sign treaties with the U.S. that would give them access to jobs making tennis shoes for people like him—Gooch.

His mind raced. Could it be that all of this was a good-natured prank from Sugar Valley's rivals, Muhammad X. Bin Laden High? A gentle poking in response to the hilarious cross-burnings, hangings in effigy, the "Die, Jungle Bunnies" graffiti that appeared one night on all the school's buildings? He smiled. Of course they must have had help, blond help, because he couldn't imagine those Napster-headed ho's coming up with such an elaborate plot on their own.

"I'm sorry about Strange Fruit Theme Day," he said. "But you gotta admit, the Peachanaorange was pretty strange fruit. Not that I would know what strange fruit is. Look, guys, can't we be white about all this? Forgive and forget, huh? Guys? Bros?"

Columbus Lincoln was nearly on top of him before Gooch realized his mistake. They were not all just going to get along. They had hostile intentions. He could tell they were hostile because of the deep rumble of voodoo drums all around him, the circle closing in, the misshapen masks glowering over him, as they poked him with long spears and chanted something in a primal jungle language.

"You guys are bad sports!" whined Gooch. "Just 'cause Sugar Valley kicked your ass at Death Ball, you don't have to get all 'in my face' about it. We dominated, fair and square. You lost! Man the fuck up, bitches!"

But they were not having any of it.

***

This was pain quite unlike anything Gooch had ever experienced. Relentless, remorseless suffering.

Like the time—but his life had been so adversity-free, so charmed, that he couldn't remember a time like it.

Except, wait, the time he'd been rejected by that little Hollywood slut in biology class when he tried to copy her notes.

The one he'd wanted so badly to pee on. Stream golden showers over. Dazzle with Gooch's special lemonade.

Nobody had ever rejected Sugar Valley High's Death Ball hero, denied him a reasonable request, even the smallest favor. Who did she think she was, anyway? She wasn't that special. But she'd made him burn. And nobody burned the Goochman.

That was the closest Gooch had been to a real setback in 18 years. Until now.

Now was living death. Castrated, headless, and set loose in a dense, humid jungle only to be captured and roughly used by zombies with appallingly large members.

Treated like a little bukkake boy. Made to do unspeakable things with unmentionable commie liberal foreigners in a setting his favorite Hot Fox pundit, Fran Cooter, would describe as "fucktarded."

And then released again, slathered with zombie spunk, crashing through rubbery foliage that had its own will.

At least they'd left him his other limbs. He imagined himself on the Death Ball field and took the special Berserker stance that always drew gasps of amazement, wonder and toxic shock from the stands, his elbows punching laterally like pistons, shredding leaves and vines and finally, with a sense of huge relief, bursting out of the jungle.

He could smell the ocean very close.

And heard the zombies tromping through the jungle right behind him.

Gooch estimated that the ocean was about 15 yards away. If he ran very fast, he might be able to get to the water before the zombies got in their sloppy seconds. And thirds. And fifths. And…

"Fuck this shit!" screamed Gooch.

It then occurred to him that he didn't have a head.

So how was he screaming? And thinking? He had a vague sense that his head, wherever it was, had been manipulated, scrambled, digitally patched into another narrative, rejected, set aside, replaced with a succession of unwieldy proxies, flash-frozen, stored in a man-sized fridge with an Irish-Kenyan U.S. President, taken out, used for masturbation by an 8-foot-tall glam rock hermaphroditic somnambulist trance-killer, patched into a Death Ball game, bounced around in a locker room, had pictures taken with it wearing a frilly pair of undies, kicked into a corner to gather dust, and then transformed after unquiet dreams into a special cockroach-sconed dildo.

It was ever so slightly exciting. And if Gooch still had his 12-inch, he might have had wood. But the zombies were gaining. There was no time to reflect, head or no head, cock or no cock.

Stripped of pride, dignity, self-assurance and even the last vestige of Death Ball attitude, Gooch paddled out into the blood-warm ocean.

The zombies followed.

***

Now that he was one of them, the zombies left Gooch alone.

To say he was traumatized would be the understatement of the millennium. Treading water and leaking a steady stream of blood from his ass, Gooch could barely summon the energy to struggle on.

His wood was missing, his head had been replaced with a girl's, and though the girl's head in turn still held Gooch's brain and thought Gooch's thoughts, these were of an inferior quality. Not that he had prided himself on his thinking skills.

No, that was for the nerds, who couldn't get a date and thought an evening watching reruns of *Dr. Who* on the BBC and writing fan-fic about Harry Potter characters was about as exciting as life ever got. Gooch liked to spend his evenings being serviced by the entire Death Ball cheerleading squad—go Aryans!—while watching videos (featuring himself) in which he led the team to blood-spattered victory. Now, he had been reduced to nothing. Less than nothing.

He would be lucky if he got a gig as a water boy for a freak show. He would be lucky to consider himself one of the 47% of gay retards driving around in their womb-mobiles. He would be lucky to be anything other than he was, which was a horribly fucked-up mutant.

Behind him, the water was boiling with zombie-shark action. Through Tiffany Tiffany's eyes, Gooch watched unlikely penetrations and awesome acts of swallowing. A cloud of mingled zombie/shark spunk, rotten zombie jissom horribly swapped together with shark essence, blossomed like a corpse-born flower.

Taking advantage of the distraction, Gooch summoned all his strength and began to swim away from the scene. He dove beneath the sperm cloud and then up and around in a wide sweep, heading back to land.

He could almost believe he was back on the Death Ball field, bearing a rival's head for the pike. He could hear the crowd's roar, practically taste the percussive impact, the wet "sploot" sound as neck stalk met metal and he raised the gory trophy high. Every yard gained from the zombie/shark orgy took him further and further away from his pain. So he had a girl's head now. So what? At least he was still blond.

IX.

"Crap!" said Brittany, shaking her cell phone. Maybe it didn't work in the movie world. But how could that be? Unless it was a movie prop, in which case she hoped the audience heard her having a long, sophisticated convo with her analyst about her Daddy issues. Brittany was pretty sure they added stuff like that in post-production. The whole scene was so sketchy, all she could be was pretty sure about a lot of things.

She hated not being in control. Or having a nice, strong, blond guy who had all the answers, like Daddy. Granted, Daddy didn't have many answers, but he did have strong family values, for which Brittany was super-grateful. She was so proud of her dad. Unlike some others she could mention, he had never put out his hand and asked for a government handout once. And he refused to pay for the support of people who didn't want to work, who sat around on their stoops and drank malt liquor all day and whined that the government should enable their crude and despicable habits. Like some of the characters around her, on the street, in the alleyways, perched on top of buildings, scratching themselves, covered with insects. Drooling. Indolent.

And everywhere.

Brittany was also proud that, thanks to her Daddy, she had never been forced to ask for help either. She hoped that when she was way older a guy exactly like her Daddy, strong, commanding and sure of himself, would keep her in the lifestyle she was accustomed to, and give her tons of presents, and leave her alone when she felt like being a bitch. And treat her like a princess. An old-fashioned, brutal guy with a six-pack, short hair and a nice car.

That wasn't asking too much, was it? Brittany didn't think so. She would be happy to spend the rest of her life in her pretty pink bedroom, with the posters of hot guys and pumped-up cars, listening to Lash Rumble on the radio, secure in her safety from any dependence on big government, which according to Daddy was way, way too big and needed to be slimmed down.

Daddy would know how to handle this situation, keep his princess safe, and give a mighty ass-kicking to all the dusky, stinky, sweaty, grotties she kept seeing. It was almost like they ran the country. The whole country, not just a well-fenced part of it. Something was very amiss at the Circle-K.

She looked around for an Ahab's Coffee. Even in a movie, or especially in a movie, there had to be an Ahab's. After all, weren't they everywhere on the planet? And a movie set was no exception. Only maybe this wasn't a set. It was—she wrinkled her brow in an unusual attempt to concentrate—an alternate dimension. Ugh. That was so nerdy. Like those gross boys of size that hung out at Zapple Comix and shouted about dragons and hit points. They were so immature. She hated even thinking about them. But at a time like this she almost wished she knew one of them, at least well enough to ask him about the alternate dimension thing. Nerds could be useful in a very limited sense, if they knew things like math and science and didn't bore her too much with their weird, lame, boring socially inept babble about vast Cyclopean cities beneath the sea.

The nearest thing to an Ahab's looked more like an Arab, which scared Brittany, because Daddy said they were all terrorists and prayed to something called a Gee Hod. It was a little hole in the wall—actually, literally a hole in the wall. Brittany told herself to be brave and investigate. She needed an espresso and to get her bearings.

"Is anybody, like, there and stuff?" she asked, peeping through the hole. She caught a flash of very tall non-blonds shuffling around. There was a group of them in the corner chanting words that sent a sharp tingle of fear through her skinny, stacked, super-hot bod. She smelled smoke—evil, acrid, cancer-causing smoke, and her boobs felt like they were crawling with the "C" word. Maybe this was a bad idea.

"Hello?"

For some reason her ass-tat was pulsing, even though she'd had it done a year ago, secretly, while Daddy was away on a business trip. The ass-tat told her things, not always coherent or reliable things, but at least it didn't just sit there on her lower back like a useless welfare queen. It was weird to think of her body parts that way, but she tried to be scientific and rational and believe in miracles. Which was also weird. She wished she were back in Sugar Valley and if Godaddy granted her super-special wish she would never, ever, ever, binge and purge again, would listen to Lash with renewed fervor, and try to emulate the flawless girls on the Carpathians.

But she'd been spotted. It was too late for denial or pretending. She would actually have to interact with one of them. Or several. A whole pack of them.

***

"Where am I?" asked Brittany. She found herself on a lab bench, strapped down tight. She vaguely recalled that the Arabs had given her something to drink, which must have been laced with goofy powder, because there was no way she had volunteered to be the girl who gets experimented upon, least of all by some horrid dyke-domme like the one who was palpating her tits.

"Hello?" she asked. "Could you give me, like, some kind of explanation? What am I doing here?"

"Solare, the needle—quickly. This one needs to be put down like a five-legged puppy."

Brittany felt a sudden sting in her arm, and then everything went blurry.

When she woke up, she was lying in a strange bed. Across from the bed was a mirror. Looking herself up and down to see if anything was different, she satisfied herself that she was the same hot, pretty girl who had arrived at the theater hoping the movie wouldn't be totally lame. But it was worse than lame. It was a nightmare she couldn't awaken from.

Her head was completely wrapped in bandages. She couldn't figure it out. Unless—unless the bitch had done heinous, wrong, gross plastic surgery on her! Part of her wanted to go back to sleep and hope that the movie would change into one of those nice chick flicks with the handsome vampire guys who don't really want nooky because they're more gay than anything, and then she could have a nice small snack—maybe just a little salad—exfoliate, and go back to sleep.

The other part was curious beyond anything. Tugging a flap from the mummy wrap, Brittany loosened the cloth gradually, then faster, as she saw some very familiar features arise before her.

And gasped, and screamed, because the features were not her own. They belonged to her arch-rival, Tiffany Tiffany St. Tropez.

All of a sudden she felt a thick pressure against her ass. At the same moment, her head vanished.

X.

Viola Flesh sat down at the editing bay and reviewed her options. The randomizing feature she'd built into the sims had generated so many choices it made her head spin.

Making her head spin was also among the choices at her fingertips, but there were more delicious options available.

She could dial into the narrative at the point where the headless, castrated body of Gooch, newly zombified, awoke in the water to find itself being sodomized by a shark. Although a head was not strictly speaking necessary for Gooch to experience all the horrors attendant upon this multiple violation of his manhood—consciousness being non-local, and a phantom, proxy head would always do—Viola considered patching Brittany's head into the mix.

Currently Brittany was wandering through a hallucinogenic dreamscape in Room 666, her hair on fire and her ass tat leading the way through a forest of Surprise Pussy dolls in domme dress. Were she to suddenly awaken as a male torso only to be cruelly fucked by a shark, it might unhinge what was left of her sanity. Or not.

There were certain inherent limits Flesh was forced to observe. Limits framed by the relative psychic evolution of the guinea pigs. Although she could stretch their minds like taffy, she couldn't necessarily put them back intact.

And then there was Tiffany Tiffany. Poor Tiffany Tiffany, the girl so nice they'd named her twice. The sufferings of that one that had been so extreme, complex, perplexing and ghastly, even Viola felt a twinge of guilt as she rehearsed the things she'd done to Ms. St. Tropez.

Dr. Flesh plucked another opium-tainted cigarette from the packet of Egyptian smokes, lit it and sucked the smoke deep into her lungs. She was so restless. And bored. She needed very badly to have an orgasm.

She wondered if the present course—endless, extreme, surreal revenge against her perceived enemies—wasn't merely the function of an unhappy childhood. First her crazy mom, then the priest, then the discovery of Chaosian porn, then the delvings into forbidden books of Dark Magick, her brief relapse into a guilt-soaked private version of Catholicism, rereading the books, finding even greater solace in those passages that dealt with the summoning of the Gods of Gokkun and the Rites of the Bowl, then finding the old Super 8 camera in the attic and making her dolls do terrible, perverted things with stop-motion animation, and her resolve to become a medical deviate slash occult film-maker, bloggers be damned.

She needed more opium-tainted cigs. And she really needed to get off. Meanwhile the guinea pigs were still battling invisible enemies.

Maybe she should just cut them loose. Let them return to their mall-crawling lives, their small salads, their triumphs on the Death Ball field. What did it matter to her if they remained shallow xenophobes with all the intelligence of faux fur? She might exercise a little compassion. Or pity. Take up Zen. The dharma path. Dissolve her ego into the white radiance of nirvana. Do some Pilates. Adopt an African child. Get more cosmetic plastic surgery.

Or she could just say fuck it, flip the switch, link the sims directly into the narrative, put the Randomizer on Fully Fucked Up Scramble Mode, surprise Solare in its sleep and get some hermaphrodite action.

***

Dr. Flesh strode through the theater, noting the distinct, wet details. You complete me, she thought. Quite literally. For had her life not become a movie? A movie without a plot, with total unknowns as actor, incorporated, sucked into the wet innards of a biological machine: a camera, projector and film in one. A Camjector.

It was unfortunate that her audience had been plucked from their seats and sewn into the fabric of the Reality Stack, because that left her with nobody to hear her triumphant speech. The one that began "they called me mad at the university."

The Eyeball Bondage headsets were all that remained of the audience. Their essence had been captured and transferred to the biofilm, leaving hunks and smears of glop on the seats. Some residual slime covered the floor of the theater and she nearly slipped several times as she surveyed the scene.

The Reality Stack had delimited the contours of the electrical body and boiled down the flesh to a convenient packet that could be transformed into discrete streams of bioessence. Perhaps some day she would figure out a way to eliminate the waste, the reek of putrefaction, the rotting lumps, gobbets and nubbins to which her machine had reduced them.

But the process had been mostly smooth. Most important, it had worked. Every truly genius innovation in science and technology had its casualties, and if this was the worst of it, she had triumphed indeed.

But something was missing. Solare.

Which led to her first moment of doubt. It wasn't possible, no, she couldn't have been so caught up in the movie that she had allowed her somnambulist hermaphroditic assistant/sex toy to be consumed, subsumed into the ravening maw of the biomachine.

Or had she?

Loud rumbling noises came from the speakers. Static twined with something deeper, lower, a subliminal *killkillkill* message that repeated at different speeds and resolved into a high-pitched whine that had Dr. Flesh clutching her ears in pain.

On the screen, terrible things were happening. Key scenes, taken at random, trotted through variations of stunning complexity. A tall woman in a laboratory coat strode towards the camera and winked. It was her, Dr. Flesh's doppelganger, the proxy she had placed in the narrative stream to direct the movie from inside.

Which seemed like a good idea at the time. Only it raised several questions: first, as she herself had stepped out of the movie, what did that make her? Was her doppelganger the real Dr. Flesh? Or had it transformed into her while she was nodding off at the wheel? Was all of this still a movie, in which case another Dr. Flesh sat yawning at some fantastic editing bay, avoiding work with SexyFandom.com and subtly jacking it? Moreover, with all the egg-born doppelgangers sliming around, would she ever be able to distinguish between the original, the original duplicate and their kinfolk?

And who was thinking these thoughts—her real self, the movie proxy self, or the other, lazy, masturbating self, the one who had created this monstrous scenario in the first place?

The Camjector was rising on new, wet legs and screaming the scream of the mandrake, as it burst through the projection booth and fell into the last seats, still smeared with collapsing cells and the rot with no name. It wore cowboy boots, a tall black hat, a duster, clutched Hitler Youth daggers in its black leather gloves, and was growing steadily in width and height.

Dr. Flesh panicked. Solare was still missing, and the Camjector was gaining on her, taking rapid steps through the center aisle and speaking in a polyglot of dubbed movie languages.

"Don't hurt me," said Dr. Flesh in a last-ditch effort to assume control. "I'm part of you. If you kill me, you'll kill yourself."

"That's bullshit," roared the Camjector through the house speakers.

She had to admit that the creature had a point.

"I know you want to click your stiletto heels and wake up in the Okay State," said the Camjector. "But you know what? It's not gonna happen."

"Damn," thought Dr. Flesh, who had been counting on that maneuver as an option.

"This is what happens when you treat acid as just another breakfast cereal. Didn't anybody tell you that drugs are bad for you? Didn't anybody ever teach you to just say no?"

Viola had to admit that although that instruction had been attempted, it just didn't take.

"You thought you were too good for the simple, durable claims of consensual reality. You took chaos as a starting point, as opposed to a very scary, off-limits taboo area man was not meant to explore. You wanted to be Frankenstein 2.0, the Postmodern Prometheus. You scoffed at the delicate but essential boundaries between fact and fiction, dream and reality, flesh and spirit."

Viola had to admit the creature's point there too.

"Look on thy works, ye mighty, and despair!" said the Camjector, opening the duster and revealing a capacious set of tits.

"Damn, them's good eatin,'" thought Viola, unaccountably. The creature's tits would do credit to any fertility goddess. They looked like they could carry enough milk to supply any number of mutant, hybrid children."

"Like what you see?"

Viola nodded.

"Want to tittie-fuck me?"

Viola nodded again.

"Look," said the Camjector. "I don't have endless time to bandy words. This is the stirring climax where creature confronts creator. Only now the roles have been reversed. And reversed again. Damn, even I don't know what the fuck you've created."

"It's a mystery," said Viola philosophically. Experimentally, she clicked her stiletto heels twice and thought of Leatherface.

"How's that working for you?" said the Camjector.

"Not…so…good," said Viola. "That, or Oklahoma is a little different than I remembered it."

The Camjector's twins shot forth fiery beams, drilling Dr. Flesh straight through the forehead with dream plasma.

"You twat!" she screamed. "That really hurt."

"You said pain was unreal, that nothing was real. So why are you whining like a little bitch?"

"I am not whining like a little bitch," said Dr. Flesh defiantly. "Who made who made who made what…look, can't we just sit down and talk this over, irrational adult to mutant creature?"

"What, you mean like over coffee?" roared the Camjector.

"Yeah, kind of like that," said Dr. Flesh. "Game?"

"It's a fucking stupid idea, and anticlimactic into the bargain. The time for talking this over with a nice cup of java has long past. Time to die, you medical deviant!"

She had to admit the words had a nice pulp fiction quality to them. It was unfortunate, then, that she herself had ruptured the boundary lines separating pulp fiction from squishy medical fact.

The Camjector opened the duster to reveal a set of massive lungs, like an accordion file. The lungs crackled and wheezed.

From inside the duster's lining, dozens of transparent scrotal sacs depended. Within them could be seen flash-frozen images from the movie: Gooch being impaled on the Great White's two-pronged spear, Tiffany Tiffany's soul being sought in vain, as she screamed for small salads through the pump gag, the elaborate lengths to which the blogger had been driven when he realized that snarky reviews can have lethal consequences, and an oddly tranquil fantasy sequence featuring a small boy, a balloon and liquid acid.

The sacs burst, heaving the contents onto the lab floor. Dr. Flesh watched with fascinated horror as the products of her mad science crawled, wriggled and slithered towards her, a spreading pool of monstrosities.

But the worst was yet to come.

Behind the spurting sacs lay a curtain. The curtain ripped open to reveal an unusually large coffin, built as though to contain the form of a somnambulist hermaphrodite hench-thing.

"Meet my not-so-little fiend," exulted the Camjector through the wall-to-wall speakers.

The coffin lid yawned.

"Solare?"

Solare leapt down from the coffin, bearing a telescoping spear.

As if that wasn't bad enough, Viola felt the twin terrors of projectile vomit and explosive diarrhea churning within her guts.

"You aren't seriously going to…" began Solare as Viola clutched her belly and raised an index finger in the universal "be with you in a second" hand signage.

The vomitus was rank, copious and extensive, spattering the sleepwalking hermaphrodite with a foul, yellow-green goop. At the same time her bowels let loose, ripping a hole straight through her frilly French panties and smearing the inside of her erstwhile pristine lab coat with watery shit.

It seemed like insult to injury, but Solare added a painful eyeball spearing to the mix.

***

A movie for beautiful people only, *Dr. Flesh* stars some truly unmemorable, generic, highly modular characters and extraordinary synthetics. Retrospectively it may be viewed as yet another version of *The Hands of Orlac* outfitted for rugged adventure with elements of *The Most Dangerous Game* and spliced into a jelly aquarium.

The idiotically simplistic plotline features zombies, a zombie doctor, sex change operations and organ transplants. It is revolting, sickening and putrid in almost every fly in aspic except one.

Don't see *Dr. Flesh* if you've just eaten of the fruit of the tree of the knowledge.

XI.

Bilge started awake.

He'd missed the end of the movie, but he generally fell asleep earlier, passing into the unquiet sleep of the blogger.

In his dream, *Dr. Flesh* was not only the biggest pile of crap he'd ever had the misfortune to sit through as a non-paying audience member, it was maybe the worst movie ever conceived. How Viola had garnered funds for it was the biggest mystery of all, considering her record. But she had done it, finally. If she wasn't permanently banned from the industry and made to suck eggs on an irregular pumpkin-metaphysical prison planet, there was simply no justice.

He peeled off the headset and tossed it in the aisle, looked around for the nearest exit and made a beeline for it, the review already forming itself in his mind.

"If you hated its precursor and abhorred the one before that, if you think Dr. Flesh should go back to medicine and stay far, far away from cinema, *Reality Stack* will not change your mind one iota. If anything, it will confirm what you already suspected— that Viola Flesh is a bloated non-talent, a pretentious pseudo-artiste whose dreams of grandeur are belied by her truly puke-worthy efforts. Although this blogger must admit that the technology employed is truly spectacular, it is utterly wasted on an incoherent plot, inane and unbelievable characters, and cinematography straight out of Ed Wood's ecstatic nightmares."

Bilge walked out into the street. The neighborhood between Bunuel Street and Jodorowsky Avenue was still as creepy as he remembered it. Nothing had changed under the sun. Now to find his car and return to Redundant Beach where he shared tight quarters with Flopsy, Mopsy, Hairy, Belchy and the Fart Twins, also known as Coven of Superfans.

"Oh my god, that was so weird!" said a voice behind him.

He turned around. There she was, the girl from the audience, the one without the really sexy ass-tat. Off-screen, she still looked good. She was trying to catch her reflection in a window, patting herself down and probably reassuring herself that she was back to small-salad proportions.

"Who's that weirdo?" she asked her companion, Matt Gooch, who was escorting her and her former rival, Brittany Lapierre, back to his home in Sugar Valley for a crank-fueled threesome.

"Who do you mean?" asked Gooch.

"That pervy, hairy guy...I think he writes a blog?"

Bilge bristled. He was standing five feet away and they were talking shit about him. Like he was invisible, or utterly devoid of feelings. Or not worth the effort involved with dignifying his humanity. A thing, snark-bait.

"I loved the conceptual innovations," said Gooch. "I think Flesh has really captured the zeitgeist, you know? Our sense that identity is no longer a fixed structure, that it participates in culture and to a certain extent is embodied in culture."

What?

"I totally agree," said Tiffany Tiffany, hanging off his arm. "I didn't mean weird in the bad way, more like the Freudian sense, you know, *unheimlich.* The uncanny."

"Hot *and* perceptive," said Gooch. "We are so going to have that crank-fueled three-way and maybe write our blogs afterward? What did you think, Brittany?"

"I totally agree with Tiffany Tiffany," said Brittany. "It was definitely weird in the best sense possible. Totally."

So now everyone's a critic, thought Bilge. If he wasn't experiencing it himself he might think this was just another bizarre narrative turn in the movie. But now, come to think of it, the movie had felt *more real* than this did, which meant...what...that they were either still in the movie, or the movie had succeeded in cloning and amping up the signal of the formerly real..."oh yeah, totally Baudrillian," Brittany was saying. "Hyper-real."

He could have sworn the three were just empty-headed hormone bags from Sugar Valley, but now they were talking like they'd just stepped off the pages of *Cahiers du Cinema.* Could it be that he, Bilge, was the irrelevant one? Just another not particularly bright loud-mouth with an opinion?

He was starting to feel thinner, less substantial. As he walked towards the parking lot, he realized that his body was evaporating. Shrinking. Although he still felt the cold air and could smell the stench of the city, there was less and less of him the further he went. By the time he had reached his car, he was almost completely invisible.

"Hey," said Gooch, 15 feet behind him. "Was that Nathan Bilge?"

"Who?" asked Tiffany Tiffany.

"Oh yeah, Bilge," chuckled Brittany. "Couldn't write his way out of a paper bag. A total geek with grandiose delusions."

"How many readers does he have now?" asked Gooch.

"Maybe his mom," said Tiffany Tiffany.

The three exploded with laughter as Bilge completed his descent into obscurity.

Doctor Flesh Part Two: Pink Holocaust

I.

Vice President Duke Charnel clawed his way out of a fresh hole in the White House lawn like a deranged marmot. When he had entirely emerged, he was clad in an SS officer's hat, a butcher's apron and a jockstrap, all made of black leather. His body was white as soap from years spent underground, and as the mid-morning sun splashed against his backside, President Bermuda O'Clodder winced, noting the shadowed craters of acne scars on the Veep's buttocks.

Charnel began chucking rocks at the President's window.

O'Clodder looked down, wiped the sleep crust from his eyes, cursed whatever chemical cocktail was in his system when he chose his Vice President, rushed down the stairs two at a time, burst out the door, grabbed Charnel and pulled him inside.

"Jesus, man, what is wrong with you? Have you been tunneling again?"

"No time to talk," said Charnel. "We'll have to pull it. Now."

"Pull what?"

"My finger. Listen, you arrogant sack of shit. You're lucky I've been in charge of the shadow presidency all this time. Otherwise I'd be talking to a robot duplicate. Hell, I oughta cyborg you right now just for questioning me. Who do you think faked your birth certificate? I spilled blood for you, Bermuda. Literal blood. Not my own, of course, but lots of the red, red krovvy. So when I say 'pull it,' I mean, put the secret plan in operation. Or did you really enjoy living in my man-sized freezer?"

"It was chill," mumbled O'Clodder, shivering involuntarily at the memory. "But I went to school in Sugar Valley. It's a great community. Beautiful, well-kept lawns. And the draperies—just bursting out with passementerie. Thousands of dollars' worth."

"Oh, save your interior decorating expertise for someone who cares," said Charnel. "Where's the black box?"

"You mean Mrs. O'Clodder?"

"No, you fool. The box with the button that if you push it, sets in motion the codes of utter devastation."

"Fine, I'll get the box. Shouldn't I make some sort of public announcement, though? Maybe we should warn them, you know, so they can clear the aorta—I mean area— before we detonate the UltiBomb."

"No time, no time!"

"That's what you always say, Charnel. You're like that fucking bunny in *Alice in Wonderland*. But there should be time, dammit. There should always be time to pause, contemplate, reflect and reconsider before an act of this gravity and magnitude, affecting the lives of millions of people. We're not murderers, after all, despite what you wrote in your autobiography."

Charnel snorted.

"Maybe just a Twitter?"

"Okay, you get one Twitter. Make it good. Then we pull it."

"Sometimes I wonder if you have any soul at all, Charnel."

The Vice President smiled, revealing a mouth full of jagged, blackened teeth. "It's a good thing you're not the real President and never will be. You're much too naïve for the job."

The President opened his laptop. "Wait, I have a ton of messages on Facefuck. Let's see—oh, this is good. 'Hi, I saw your profile and I love it. Here's a link to some pix LOL. Giggle. Maybe we can get together some time.' You see that, Charnel? Damn, this girl is hot. And she's barely wearing anything. Just a teensy weensy strip of cellophane. What should I say?"

"That's exactly what I was getting at just now, Bermuda. The naivete. The utter simplicity of your mind! That's not a real live girl, it's a bot. A bot! You've been too busy staring at big hippie tits to see the crazy behind them."

The President looked crestfallen. "Yeah well, some of those hippie chicks really got it going on, you know? 'Drivin' that train, high on cocaine...'" O'Clodder's a capella version of the Dead classic was both off-key and highly inappropriate, a fact which the President immediately realized as he trailed off and lapsed into an embarrassed silence. "Um, anyway, I'm going to post a status update. Just a little one. Some good friends and supporters of this administration live in Sugar Valley."

"You'll be the death of me, Bermuda," said Charnel. "But go on. Tweet your Tweet. Share your status. If that's what it takes for you to focus on the real business at hand."

"What should I say, just..."

"Do I have to do everything around here? Just say..." Something flickered behind Charnel's eyes. Were those feelers? The President suspected flashbacks from his days at Accidental College. If his senses weren't betraying him, then Charnel wasn't, strictly speaking, human.

For a moment it was as though he could see right through the man, and what he saw was extraordinary in its ugliness and sheer perversion. Smoking diodes, twisted circuitry, heaps of rubble with bugs crawling through them.

Charnel suddenly lurched towards the President and clamped his hands around his neck. "What did you see, dude?"

"Nothing...I saw nothing. Carry on," said the President distractedly. "We'll sort this out later."

"It's probably nothing more than a TSA—Transient Schematic Attack."

"Yeah, that's it," said the President. "Maybe we should just get this thing over with?" There was no use arguing with the Veep when he got like this.

Charnel smiled and sticky wings clapped on his lips. "Indeed."

***

O'Clodder now found himself in a pentagonal chamber deep in the bowels of the White House, a place he only knew about from rumors subsequently squelched and their originators redacted. Screens covered every wall with live video feeds from various ongoing operations of the shadow government, as well as a generous selection of fetish porn.

Charnel bent over a machine that resembled a speaker's podium, complete with microphone. He cleared his throat and leveled a frosty gaze at the President.

"I saw where you went, right there."

"Huh?"

"You were thinking about muff. Hairy twat. Jungle bush."

"I was not, and how dare you insinuate…" O'Clodder sputtered. "I am the fucking President, and this is a very grave and serious moment. To imply that my mind is on anything but the crisis in Sugar Valley is beyond the realm of insult. I…"

"You can protest as much as you like, but you forget about the microchip."

"What microchip?"

"Come and take a look."

O'Clodder reluctantly joined Charnel and gazed over his shoulder at the podium. Without a doubt, the display screen was flush to bursting with quim. "Well," O'Clodder said, "that proves nothing. Anybody with a Supranet link can pull up 'Girls with Natural Papaya' or any related site. Not that I'm familiar with those…ahem…under certain conditions, the President is privy to esoteric, um, concerns that may or may not affect the body politic."

"Oh really," said Charnel. "I want you to look carefully. This isn't just any follicular snatch page. Check out the design in her foliage. A peace symbol. You can see where some of the blonde hairs are lighter than the background. It's actually touchingly artful, from a detached aesthetic place, I mean. Too bad that isn't where your head is at, my friend. *Voila*, a slice of presidential brain gone crazier than a Coco Puffs addict over fleecy hippie vajay."

"And?"

"I rest my case. As you yourself have so self-righteously indicated, we do face an unprecedented crisis, a danger to democracy here and perhaps everywhere democracy can plant its tiny tendrils, and you've gone off the rails for pacifistic pilose pussy!"

"At least I'm not a clown-fucker," muttered the President under his breath.

"I beg your pardon?"

"You heard me. I'm not the only one with microchip-implanting capability. So maybe we both have a little something, some peccadillo, some…weakness…we don't necessarily want to share with the entire world. And while I'm sure—we've done polls on this, actually—that a large number of citizens would be at least sympathetic to my particular vice, yours is different. Nobody loves a clown, and there are many that *actively hate* a clown-lover. The whole circus enterprise is rotten to the core. Mimes, jesters, jugglers, barkers, acrobats…all except those cute little bears that ride unicycles. They're cool. But the rest—meh! I ain't butting heads with no nose-bumper."

"So, ahem, to the business at hand."

"Yes, please," said O'Clodder huffily.

"You'll observe on the right the live feed from Sugar Valley. Citizens going about their business. Naughty librarians bent over behind the stacks, taking it from firemen. Fires unattended to. Er...panties tangled around the ankles. Freaks driving it balls deep..."

"None of that circus shit, Charnel."

"Oh yes, right, sorry. A pedestrian walking down the sidewalk, humming a little tune to themselves. If we listen in we can hear that the tune is cult icon Nico's version of the Doors classic, 'The End.' 'Zees ees ze ent, beyoooootiful frent, thee ent.' I actually always preferred her cover to the original. Anyway. Folks doing what folks do, completely oblivious to the gathering storm of genetic materials gone awry. Free-form DNA taking all kinds of awful shapes and configurations. Boobs with insect legs. Necks with heads sticking out the sides. Necro Fanny. And other, more complex forms. Shreck was one of ours, you know."

"Anton Shreck?"

"The very same. We were grooming him for one of the top slots in the organization. Candyman, crucifix-dealer, anything. But he went belly up when we sent him down into the Hondurican jungle to pound some curves into his flat head. Now look at him. An errand boy for a bunch of upper middle class white supremacist wannabes without the sense of a soda straw in a vat of kumquat juice."

"I'm afraid...I'm not following you."

Charnel gripped the President by the shoulders and shook him like a rag doll. "It's inspiration I'm talking about. Instinct. The holy fire. Something you lack altogether. Sometimes the only way I can explain myself is by not explaining myself. I work backwards towards the light at the end. Oh, there have been good times, but mostly—mostly the bad has shadowed me like that demon clown I left behind in Delaware. Or was it Ontario? I gorged myself on cherry pie, and look where it got me. A broken-down fool, a puppet-god gone rancid. Ridiculous and artificial. You should just kill me now, O'Clodder. Put one of those Irish-Kenyon bullets in my brain and let me die."

"Now you're just babbling nonsense, Charnel."

"That's what they called it at the university. So I kept it zipped. My genius was not for their ears. But I'm telling you now and whether you believe it later is your own affair, Shreck could have been something very different. I believed in him, his potential, and he let me down. I'm afraid he let us all down. And now, for his, and our, sins, we'll have to drop it. The UltiBomb. Right now."

The President fished in his pockets for a pair of shades. He'd seen tests of the UltiBomb conducted secretly in the Antarctic wastes, beyond the mountains of madness, where all that survived were slithering creatures with the eyes of goats and the souls of seagulls, the mere sight of which was sufficient to drive a man mad. Also, the UltiBomb was very, very loud and extremely hard on the eyes.

"Do…what you have to do," he said.

Charnel depressed a button on the podium, and a blinding flash, followed by a rumble like thunder on meth, filled the room.

***

This was no ordinary cleanup. What had seeped through the lawn, spattered the Death Ball statue that marked the entrance to Sugar Valley High—one hard blond, in perpetuity, with forcible drill-bits for all—and now lay in heaps and piles, landed slowly and softly as feathers from the land of Todd Browning, the terminal logic of all bodily fluids, the quintessence of blood, spunk, shit–slime, urine, bile, vomit–spackled pussy juice, dick cheese and other secretions only a forensic examiner could love.

One thing was clear: the usual protocols of Hazardous Waste management would have to be scrapped, perhaps entirely rethought.

"Ain't seen nothing like it before," said Jeb Smith, scratching his head and tugging down his sweat–soaked Dodgers cap. "Sure, kids today is strange, but there's strange and then there's this…looks like a whole lotta bukkake dip with maybe some gummy bears laced in there for flavorin.'"

The cleanup crew labored vigorously to separate the strata. Before any proper operations might proceed, there was the business of analyzing the task. Demarcate it, delimit it, sponge off the edges and finally, with careful and deliberate boots, wade in for the major mop job.

The top layer foamed with semen. Then came the blood plasma. After that, the mystery sauce, composed, as later discovered, of maggots whipped to the texture of churned butter, bone shards, the kind of fruit found preserved in the bellies of mummy whore rectum, phlegm, butt paste, glube, Grandma's false teeth, a formula for world peace crunched into an Origami bong, a well-read copy of the *Cultes De Goules* annotated by Bloch and Kiernan, the final integer of Pi (lightly dumbed down), a grey market VHS dub of the Joe D'Amato film *Porno Holocaust*, a packet of dried vomitus 'a la O'Neill,' the true Aleph, and a pair of filmy, cum–stiff panties.

This river of odium coursed through the gym, the cafeteria, a main hall and the room where detentions were held before halting before a black velvet painting of Death Ball Jesus and genuflecting in its own inimitable way.

Carlos Gutierrez crossed himself, made one final prayer to Santa Muerte on behalf of the cohort of cab drivers he'd worked with in TJ, clamped on his helmet and fastened it securely to the uniform, then plunged into the mire.

Random vortices corkscrewed through the hell-muck surrounding him. Gutierrez felt a strong urge to investigate, recalled too late Nietzsche's injunction about the abyss, looked long and deep, and saw reptile eyes blinking back at him.

What seemed at first like a rubber mask with a blonde wig surged to the surface. The mask's mouth opened and a piteous whine—something about small salads—tortured his ears. Ignoring this, he moved forward, pulling ahead of whatever was trying to seize his ankles and pitch him head-first into the soup. The briefing he'd been given on the operation was garbled and elliptical, interrupted by phone calls from mysterious authorities and lightning-like amendments to the plan in progress. Not that it mattered in practice—he'd seen some things back in TJ that would wither the brain stem of your average gringo, and was confident that nothing he encountered in the halls of Sugar Valley High was beyond his capacity to cope. Although he didn't care much for tentacles, by themselves or otherwise.

A bubble popped in the seminiferous blood bouillabaisse. Then a nude cheerleader whose head had been replaced by the spike-studded Death Ball and tits swapped for pompoms shot up and moved rapidly towards him. Gutierrez patted his utility belt for something he could use, or transform into, a crude makeshift weapon, found only a pair of gardening shears and assumed a fighting stance. The cheerleader's movements were jerky and erratic.

He feinted, ducked, then opened the shears as wide as he could and closed them quickly on the cheerleader's neck. The Death Ball quivered as he cut, then rolled off and sank into the muck. The neck stump squirted a fountain of green goop as the cheerleader collapsed and joined her second-generation head.

Then: the flutter of bat wings. Shadows swam down the walls. His heart began to pound, faster and faster, as he felt claws sink into an unprotected swatch of neck, followed by a sharp biting sensation. A familiar odor, pungent and musky, filtered up into his helmet.

Gutierrez blindly swatted at the bat-thing, which was now joined by its compatriots. His vision blurred, returned in crystal-sharp focus, scattered into fractal hieroglyphs and imagery from the Mayan codices. He felt an atavistic surge in his blood as the Vampussy injected him with a soothing opiate nerve agent. So this was to be his fate—a human sacrifice.

"Carlos, wake up! Wake up! You're having a terrible nightmare!"

Gutierrez opened his eyes. His wife Alicia was shaking him by the shoulders. With tentacles. He fainted again and found himself back at Sugar Valley High.

The pussybats were gone, scared off by a sound that came from the gymnasium.

Gutierrez fought the sudden urge to peel off his protective uniform and face the white man's ghosts in balls-out Aztec warrior mode. But that was just what the white man wanted, he reflected—trap him in one of their secondary institutions with Frankensteined creatures eager to turn his head into a hood ornament, then spike him with horrible claustrophobia and render him completely helpless. The green spew from the cheerleader's neck was still crusted on his helmet, making it hard to see whatever awaited him in the swamp-fog. *What Would Quetzalcoatl do?*

He forged on towards the source of the noise that had driven off the pussybats.

***

Inside the gymnasium, the muck changed color to an indifferent green glaze, on which floated bats, balls, racquets, scraps of net, helmets, mitts, wholes and portions of Sugar Valley High's athletes, complete baked elbows, partially cooked assholes skewered on sticks like kebab meat, and a few random deflated breasts. The basketball hoops on either side were stuffed with quantities of oozing genitalia, male and female, stuck together and slathered with weasel grease.

Howls, whoops, grunts, sighs and wails came from a living island of Death Team members fused with one of the coaches, Chuck Gebhardt—a mass of congealed pink flesh, like bubble gum cooking for days under a desert sun. The sounds made Gutierrez think of the creatures mired in the La Brea tar pits, moments away from oblivion and immortality as museum exhibits, their last, despairing death-cries as the hot tar sucked them under. Now, as then, denial reigned supreme.

"Sugar Valley has never lost a Death Ball match and we're not gonna start now, right guys?" Every fine, tawny hair on Gebhardt's closely-shaved head was bristling. His jaws chattered and his teeth ground together like a speedfreak in the grip of some final, apocalyptic tweek.

His pale, blue, bloodshot eyeballs slithered out on the optic nerve and shot back, like one of those ping pong paddles with the ball attached by an elastic string. His neck was sunk deep in his chest, veins throbbing and twitching. Each muscle group was defined, and tumorous clumps of sinew rose to the skin surface every few seconds.

"Right?" he roared. Then his eyeballs popped in a shower of clear gel. The coach's massive hands clawed at his sockets. A few of the team members began to sob.

"Don't be pansies! Okay, so Coach is blind. You gonna let a blind Coach set ya back? What's the matter with you? I've seen girls with more balls than you wimpy puddings."

In truth, Gebhardt had seen girls with balls over the past 48 hours, and a whole lot more. The sights had unsettled his sanity, which slunk for cover and safety in an endless, slow-motion replay of Sugar Valley's triumph over Mohammad Bin Ali High—the trophies taken, the noses and ears chewed off and swallowed, the surprisingly sweet taste of blood sipped straight from the source.

But the team was begging for a quick death. Gutierrez trembled as his hands slid over the utility belt, now discovering the blowtorch and the 9 mm. Steeling himself for the task, he administered the *coup de grace*, squirting jets of fire across every inch of the flesh island. The players and their coach set up a high, keening wail as the flames licked at their bodies, driving Gutierrez to pity and the squeezing off of a few terminal rounds from the pistol. At last, silence reigned in the gymnasium. Except for a fluttering sound. The Vampussy had returned.

He does not resist as they cluster at his neck, ripping the protective shield from his head and sinking in their claws and tubes. As he too drops into the mire, Gutierrez has a brief, prophetic flash of an afterlife. He smiles grimly, then slips out of sight, leaving only bubbles.

II.

Viola Flesh smiled as she wiped the glass countertop of the concession display case with a moist towel. The reception for her follow-up to *Reality Stack, Ledger's Jizzlobber Vs. The Sultan of Weird in 4D*, had earned epic acclaim from everybody except Nathan Bilge, whose snarky, vindictive critique of *Reality Stack* only served to maximize sales of the home version. Now housewives in Middle America were getting a taste of the ultimate interactive cinema experience, their copies of *500 Shades of Man Gravy* gathering dust. *Time* magazine hailed Dr. Flesh as "the new queen of avant-garde film," and her work was a surprising smash at every level. Bilge flatly turned down Flesh's offer of a cameo in *Ledger's Jizzlobber,* and a Twitter war ensued.

The special effects for the new movie involved a literal materialization, and the theater floor was thoroughly spattered and smeared with globs of jissom, which had begun to rot—a sickly-sweet protein-bleach odor that permeated the building. Flesh made a note to either hire a cleanup crew or advertise for spunk fetishists that might be willing to do the job for free, and pay her for the privilege.

After wiping the countertop, she opened the display case to check on snack levels. There was wicked candy in profusion, edible replicas of Harry O'Brien, aka Jizzlobber, and his arch-enemy, The Sultan of Weird. Crunchy, tangy, zippy, sweet n' salty, stretchy, chocolaty, gooey, sour, in tubes and boxes and bags and other delivery systems. By far the runaway audience favorite was the Jizzlobber in a hard candy shell with a creamy center that kind of spurted in your mouth. Flesh made a mental note to restock that one. When suddenly there came a rapping, as of something gently…busting some rhymes.

"We're closed!" she shouted at whoever or whatever had chosen this moment to interrupt her work. Then she saw who it was: Death Cat and Storm Crow, both standing outside the theater. Death Cat had gone to seed, packed on the pounds, and his mariachi jacket didn't quite fit him any more. Storm Crow had some kind of VR goggles on and was reacting to invisible stimuli, flapping her wings and hopping up, down and sideways. Sighing, Dr. Flesh unlocked the door and let them in.

"You might have at least texted," she said. "I didn't expect you guys till next month, when we start shooting your movie. What's up with you two?"

Death Cat scratched his armpits, sniffed them and shrugged. "It's her," he said. "She's got a bad Tide habit. She doesn't even like to do the old flesh and feathers roll. Just look at her."

Dr. Flesh observed that Storm Crow's feathers were fuzzed, cracked and split along the cartilage, sparse to the point of balding in some places. "All she does all day long is log on to her RPG and shoot Tide," Death Cat added plaintively.

"And this involves me how, exactly?"

"We thought maybe you could shoot us a little advance, get the old girl on her claws again."

"What happened to the money I gave you last month?" asked Dr. Flesh primly. "I'm not a charity foundation, and I'm not doling out funds just to keep your girlfriend in narcotics. She needs to get clean. I can always hire actors to play your parts. Neither of you even look like yourselves."

"Price of fame?" mewled Death Cat.

"Ok, look. I might have a few packets of Tide in the back, but this is the last time, understand? To tide her over, so to speak. Laundry detergent ain't cheap. As for you, you need to go on a diet."

"Does that mean you're firing us?"

Dr. Flesh softened. "You know I love you two, but you have to take care of yourselves. It's a tough business. And I get that you might have gone off the rails a little bit since your memoirs became an instant bestseller. But you can't use that as an excuse indefinitely. Look at me. I've got back-to-back smash hits with *Reality Stack* and *Jizzlobber,* but I'm not letting all that go to my head. Stay even and you'll be all right. You're the same endearing pair I met back in Texas when I was doing that show at the cantina. You haven't changed inside, but Lord, do you look gruesome on the outside."

"Then you understand," said Death Cat, batting at Storm Crow's goggles in an attempt to bring her back to open mode and some semblance of consensual reality.

"Huh, what…" sputtered Storm Crow. "Did you get the stuff? Where are we?"

"See what I'm working with here?" said Death Cat.

***

"Phone call for Dr. Shreck!"

"Can't it wait? I'm oper—I mean, I'm directing. This is a crucial scene."

"It sounds serious," said gopherfluff gal Sally Mae Ducasse, who also played a Naughty Nurse in the film and was dressed accordingly in a white vinyl uniform with a stethoscope swinging between her twin peaks. "I really think you need to take the call."

Shreck turned around, took one look at her globes, her full, fleshy lips, the corner of her mouth smeared with walrus gravy, hoisted the megaphone and said, "muffin break." Ducasse handed him the cell phone.

"Hello? I'm sorry, I don't know a Father Mallardy. A duck priest, you say? Is this some kind of fucking joke? Who is this? Oh, ok, so it's critical. I don't know who you are or what this is in reference to, but I am a very busy man and this is not a good time. Huh? What do the Karpathians have to do with it? Oh, trauma triggers. Perhaps total recall. Gotcha."

He picked up the megaphone again and barked: "we're going to try this scene once again, and this time, please try to control the flow of walrus gravy to the punk rock muppets. Drizzle lightly, *do not dump.* Got it? All right, Take 3."

Shreck's wrist had begun to ache at the point he'd severed his hand. A dam of repression broke, returning "Dr. Fuzzly," the Burp Me Melmo puppet, the bizarre lab accident, a hirsute red antagonist, a life and death struggle. The phone call brought it all back. Now the hand was a simple form-fitted prosthesis, but then—then, it was an adversary. For the past 18 years, Shreck had struggled to put Sugar Valley and Operation True Blonde in some deep pocket of his unconscious, but the whole ugly scene had begun to brim over the sides again. And all because of that reality show. *The Karpathians.*

Of course he'd seen the episode the duck priest had alluded to, in which Karsten Karpathian had a complete "blondeover" on a set recalling the high points of German Expressionist film, heavy on *Caligari* and *Metropolis.* Apparently, this was sufficient to spark memories in the women Shreck had impregnated through the offices of his heavy metal Frankenstein monster, memories that threatened to rip the social fabric of Sugar Valley a brave new one. For Shreck, it was over and done with ages ago, but for these women, the nightmare had only begun. Why the duck priest had become involved, and the extent of Shreck's current responsibility towards the elite enclave, were mysteries that eluded him. He refocused on the scene, or tried to.

Only one aspect of the job he'd done in Sugar Valley still bothered him. An aspect that had several facets, all troubling. After weeks of trial and error to rival Thomas Alva Edison and his fucking filaments, Shreck had taken advantage of the discovery of Italian scientists—free-form DNA—which he then injected his stud monster with. The stud monster had forthwith impregnated the brood mares of the True Blonde Cohort, and as far as Shreck knew, the results had been successful. The women had borne mindless twats, conservative, greedy and ultra-shallow in the cradle and ready now at the age of 18 or thereabouts to receive their own treatments. Shreck had left that to his successor, apparently the duck priest.

But—and this one contingent fact made his megaphone shake in his hands and his voice quiver—the beta tests he'd run, the living sims created just to see the entire life cycle of the TBC, uncovered an alarming flaw. Over time, the free-form DNA grew unstable. The blondes would physically degenerate, to the point of meltdown or outright explosion. Their remains, alive in some horrible way, held the capacity to animate nonsentient life, as well as recombining to produce new creatures. Contact with the blondes during their life cycle transmitted this flaw through osmosis, a kind of high-tech vampirism. Furthermore, the terminal stage of transmission created the ultimate horror: clowns. That, more than anything else, gave Shreck the Nervous Fear.

***

The dream descends on the women of Sugar Valley like the slow drift of coke flakes in a glass globe. Grim, monotonous, inexorable, a thing of horrors and wonders. They are herded past exit signs and urged forth with cattle prods, naked, shaking, traumatized past the point where endurance expires and madness rears   its   toothy   grin.

"This girl looks downright anemic," snarls Dr. Shreck to his trembling nurse. "Start an IV, use the gokkun bowls. She needs some spunk in her veins. No wonder she keeps yammering away like   a   baby   with   a   cookie   jones."

"But   Doctor…are   you   sure?"

"Spunk and only spunk will cure what ails her," says Shreck. "Step aside, I'll do it myself." He spanks the recalcitrant arm, looking for a good vein. "Looks like I'll need to vein-douse."

Taking up an instrument familiar to the Spanish Inquisition, Dr. Shreck prods and pokes the arm until a vein stands up like an earthworm. "Sometimes you gotta go medieval on these people, it's the only way." He rams the butterfly IV in the vein, stepping back as bright arterial blood splashes his scrubs.

"Why is this patient asleep? She needs to experience this. I think we all need to experience this...radical invasive surgery without full awareness is just butchery," says Shreck under his breath. "All the great ones knew this. Nurse," he says, raising his voice, "I want you to mix some gore candy. You know, the acid, tranks, a bit of Dexedrine, a full cocktail. And keep it coming."

He steps back from the leaking patient. More blood slops on the floor. "And bring a mop. How do you expect me to work under these conditions?"

"Yes Doctor," says the nurse, bug-eyed with terror. "Anything else?"

"The puppet. I'll need the puppet."

"But the puppet is already attached."

"Oh yes, I forgot. How convenient." Dr. Shreck recalls the bizarre lab accident in which the Burp Me Melmo puppet became grafted to his left hand. "Well, then, bring Dr. Fuzzly his instruments. And an enema bag. Hop to it!"

"Who is Dr. Fuzzly?"

Shreck waved the hand-puppet imperiously. "This is Dr. Fuzzly. Or have you forgotten already?"

"I cannot countenance any of this," said Dr. Fuzzly. "Dr. Shreck, I will expose you and your nefarious practices. Your name will become a cautionary tale in the annals of medicine."

Shreck roared with laughter. "You dare lecture me on medical practice? You participated in the butt puppet protocols. Don't tell me you're having regrets now."

"Barrels of half-butt puppets tossed into vats brimming

with radioactive slop," retorted Fuzzly, "is not science. It's insanity. You must end this now!"

"We are joined at the wrist," said Shreck, bringing Fuzzly up to his face. Fuzzly shrank at the sight of Shreck's rolling, bloodshot eyes, the foam gathered at the corner of his lips. "Our destinies are united!"

"Please don't spit on me," said Fuzzly.

"Spit on you? Oh, now you object to good, clean saliva? I've got half a mind to teach you some manners. Why don't we take a trip to the toilet and talk this through? I feel a fat, steaming shit coming on."

"Please, no, anything but that," shrieked Fuzzly. "I promise, I'll assist you. I'll be a good colleague. Anything. But don't stuff me up there and use my head like a dildo—please. I'll be nice. I'll change. I don't want to wind up like Turkish Burp Me Melmo."

"I don't need your excuses or your pleas," said Shreck. "You'll do what I say or I'll cut you off. I don't care how much it hurts. I will have a cooperative assistant or I will make one. Nurse, bring the micro-kit. It's time to *go balls deep.*"

"Couldn't you at least hypnotize me first?" begged Fuzzly. "For old times?"

"We go way back, don't we?" said Shreck, softening. "Remember the first time I wiped my ass with your head? Your soft, tender, fuzzy head. You gained the power of speech then."

"I was just a puppet until you came along," said Fuzzly. "Your sweet chocolate custard gifted me with consciousness."

Fuzzly remembered the rank horror of his first moments of awareness, his head encased in Shreck's asshole, his tongue plunged in feces as a steady shit-stream rained down on his head. He had determined then and there to be more than a butt-puppet. He would work nights and catch his sleep on the fly, if it meant putting himself through puppet medical school by night and hiring out his aperture by day to any hand with wallet access.

Shreck's appendage vaguely recalled his days as a Burp Me Melmo hand puppet, but that era was long gone. A bizarre lab accident, impromptu grafting, and the burps were history. So, he would become a scientist in his own right. Maybe, over time, he could convince Shreck of the error of his ways. They were, after all, joined   at   the   wrist.

"This is no time for nostalgia!" spat Shreck. "Nurse, where are   those   micro-instruments?"

"No   hypnosis?"

"No hypnosis, no treats, no gore candy. Colleagues, remember?" He shook the erstwhile puppet till it cried. "Medical warriors, wading in guts and blood with vigor and abandon. We do what needs to be done. We take risks the mundane practitioners never suspected existed. Risks born of the passion, the fever—for new limbs, new physiology, a whole new pathway to human. And you, my little butt-puppet, will cooperate."

"Ok,   but   please   stop   spitting   on   me."

III.

Gretchen Fassbinder paused over her notepad. "So you say you   have   had   the   dreams   again?"

"What?" Victoria D'Allessandro yawned. "Oh yeah, sorry, I think I must have that virus that's going around."

"Perhaps that is significant. What does the word 'virus' make   you   think   of—your   father,   for   example."

"I need to blow my nose," said Victoria.

"*Jawohl!*" said Dr. Fassbinder, writing furiously. "You know that the nose is a phallic symbol. Perhaps your desire to 'blow it,' as you say, represents a hidden wish-fulfillment fantasy involving your   buried   memories   of   incest."

"Huh? No, I have the sniffles."

It was the coke, of course, but there was no point in bringing that up. Not around Fassbinder, at any rate. The woman was like a trauma-seeking missile. She would tell her that the coke was a heap of white transference…or something…she really didn't understand what the woman saying half the time, and it wasn't just the thick Peruvian accent or whatever.

But Mr. D'Allessandro had figured out a way to cover all her appointment with the shrink, and what the hell, he was probably fucking his secretary anyway, anyway she didn't feel the slightest tinge of conscience where her husband was concerned. And while Fassbinder's inane probing never really got to the heart of the matter, at least she was good for sedative scripts. Which she needed, because the latest batch of coke was a little too speedy for her taste, and now she was jumpy all the time. No wonder her husband liked his secretary more. Besides, she was so much younger. She even looked a little like Victoria had—back in high school.

"Bastard."

"So, you dreamt that you were nearly aborted, and that brought back your anxiety complex related to your desire to suck your father's big, throbbing, cheese-caked testes…" Fassbinder took a small square of pink fabric from her top desk drawer and cleaned her horned-rim glasses, which had misted over.

"Ok, I'll tell you what I dreamed about," said Victoria, suddenly remembering the full gram she'd left in her Gooshy Fruit bag and shoved in the closet after the party with Manuel the poolboy and his freaky friends, who had taken turns and left her at the end of the night with memories, rope marks and enough spunk to make her bangs stand up on their own.

"It was funny, because all this happened years ago. I was about 17, 18. Me and some friends of mine from school got fake I.D.'s and we went to this club—the Paradise Bar and Grille, on Sundown. It's a place where a lot of rockers hang out, heavy metal guys. I was really into that at the time. There was this one singer I thought was really hot. I thought I saw him at the bar, but when I said his name, he turned around and it was someone else."

"Your   father,   perhaps?"

"Yes, my father." Victoria sighed, noting that sarcasm was lost on the therapist. "No, it was this guy I used to date. But that isn't part of the dream. Or maybe it is. Well, we had some drinks, and I was getting hammered. Man, I used to party back then. This was of course long before I met the Mister. I was throwing them back and pretty soon I couldn't stand up.

"That's when this guy came up to me. He was older, I mean, way older, and no, nothing like my father. He said he was a record producer and he liked my look. I told him to buzz off. I mean, he was creepy. He was like some kind of fucking...lizard, you know?

"But then he said he had some stuff, I don't know what it was, but I was a bit of a...coke fiend at the time. I didn't have a habit, I just liked it. Reptile Dude said this was even better than blow. I didn't really believe him, but I was up for anything, young and stupid as the saying goes. Ha ha. So we went back to this kind of V.I.P. room and he said he would be back with the shit, but he sort of disappeared. Then this other dude came up, I guess he'd been there the entire time but I wasn't really paying any attention because I wanted to get high. And find a way to stand up straight, you know? He just grabbed me by the arm like he...like he fucking owned me.

"He had this metal bracelet, I remember, with a pentagram on it. And he looked like he'd been in a lot of fights. Bruised, beat up, scars. His tattoos had tattoos over them, like when the old tattoos are fading out and the new ones don't match the old ones. But it was weird, because the scars were around his wrists and his neck, like that old Frankenstein movie. I was surprised he didn't have bolts coming out of his head, you know? I thought great, first time with my fake I.D. and I'm gonna get used and abused by the Frankenstein monster. Metal Frankenstein. Wow."

"And all of this happened in your dream?"

"Yes. I was so high that I thought, whatever, you know, I've had worse. Like the time the Death Ball team kidnapped me and took me to this outhouse in the woods. Anyway, this weird light started flashing, like a strobe light. I must have passed out, because the next thing I knew I was strapped to some kind of table. There were all these sharp instruments in a metal tray, rolls of gauze, some Magic Markers. The monster guy was drawing on me. And he was laughing like a crazed fucking…ghoul. Maybe he was writing 'Slut' on my forehead, I don't know. I don't mind though, 'cause that happens. It does! Okay, maybe not to you, but what-evs, as the kids say. The freaky producer was there too, and another guy—Smegma, I think his name was. He was kind of the background the entire time the monster was doing his business."

"And by 'his business,' you mean…sexually debauching you?"

"I guess. I'd been pretty much debauched by then. I remember it so clearly now, clearly but muted, far away and near at the same time. Like that movie with Nasty Kinky. He was dangling his thing over my mouth, and it was scarred up too, right around the base. He made me…suck it…and he forced it into the back of my throat.

"Then there was something about a half butt-puppet and radioactive rainwater in a bucket. That was Smegma. He kept coming into the room, or operating theater, whatever, with a camcorder, jacked off on the monster guy's ass—I don't think he even noticed—and then went back into another room. I was trying to take the monster's cock wherever he chose to put it, you know, being a good girl, but it was tough, it was bigger even than the Death Ball guys, and they're pretty ginormous. The record producer dude kept saying things like 'this is a sausage fest, where's the gash,' and I was like hello, girl alert. Maybe he was just trying to piss me off. Whatever. So the monster dude finishes, big money shot, then I hear this whip coming down. Hard. The record producer was wailing on the monster and the monster was sobbing and saying he deserved it or some shit! When I woke up the next day I was in my bedroom and it was like nothing had happened. My mom was unusually cheerful, for her I mean. She actually asked me what I wanted for breakfast—usually the maid took care of those things. I thought it was a little strange of her because she usually freaked out if I came home late or she knew I was fucked up. But she was humming this little song, making eggs and bacon, singing along to this sappy shit on the radio. Whatever it was, I kept thinking of Patsy Cline singing 'Crazy.' Maybe that's just me."

"So in your dream, you wake up in your own bedroom, after this night of sodomy with the Frankenstein monster, the record producer, and…Smegma?"

"That wasn't his real name, it was something like Shriek, I didn't really get it. When the monster was doing me I could see myself on this monitor they had over the lab table. The guy kept doing these zoom shots, made me dizzy looking at myself and trying to blow the monster and then the monster left, he got off and rolled off me, and there were these cartoons on the screen. Anime, I think."

"It's very interesting what you say, Victoria, because in some way your dream seems to be connected with a reconciliation with your mother. You two had become…alienated, *nicht wahr?*

Probably as a result of your Cassandra complex and your obsession with your daddy's pendulous, throbbing balls. With the big purple veins. Did he ever beat you? Did you want him to, perhaps?"

"What? No, no, no." Dr. Fassbinder's questions, as usual, focused around her own issues. Victoria tried to steer the therapist towards the question of pharmaceuticals.

"You haff, how do we say in English, med-seeking look in eyes." Fassbinder smiled, removed her glasses and gazed deeply and searchingly at her patient.

"W-what? No, what makes you think that?"

"You are bluffing. Is okay. Why I speak in pidgin English now is because of hot arousal in loins, *ja?* Constricting blood flow to brain. You have something I want, and I have something, perhaps, you can use?"

Victoria blanched. "I-I could use a little pick-me-up, now that you mention it."

"Your problems with your suppressed trauma *mit* mommy *und* daddy will require much more than 'little pick me up,' as you put it in charming American phrase. But sometimes, at least I haff read in medical literature, blockages may be unstopped by…how do we put it, girl on girl action?"

"Okay, okay," said Victoria. "But no anal whippets."

***

Courtney Steele did her best to shut out the chorus to "The Clown Dies At the End" by Bozokill, on constant mental replay since the previous night's concert. She had only half-unwillingly allowed her daughter to drag her to the show, pleased that even in her cougarish dotage she out-hottied most of the young flesh on display. Maybe they had firmer real tits, but Courtney had class, and experience. Even if she couldn't pass the pencil test without extensive help from a plastic surgeon.

But it was the Patriarch's turn to claim her attention now. Father Mallardy was pacing up and down Steele's living room, thumping his rod and staff on her plush carpet.

Nobody remembered exactly how Mallardy entered the picture. Rumor had it that he was a seventh cousin, once removed, of the uncle of one of the original founding fathers of the Sugar Valley community. Mallardy hailed from West Virginia, had shown up one day at Steele's doorstep in duck waders, brandishing a Bible and waving his foot-long grey beard in her face. She'd put him up in one of the guest rooms and made several frantic phone calls in the attempt to determine who he was and what he was there for. She was assured that Mallardy had been summoned to inspire solidarity among the members of the secret True Blonde Coalition, which had splintered off into the Total Disclosure cell and the Behead All the Bitches sect. At present, the BAB's were dominating the conversation.

"Maybe you're wondering why I'm here in this den of iniquity, here in Sugar Valley with your Death Ball Jesus and your Godless experimentation," said Mallardy. "I'm not here to preach that gospel, but to make you see the error of your ways. To renounce the spiked ball and return to the true church of the duck.

"Many times I've been out there in the swamps and marshes, many times hiding behind a blind, waiting...for a message, for the answer to my prayers, for a sign from above that the ducks are coming. I've searched my soul and sought within for a solution. Oh, how I have agonized in my heart of hearts. And you know what I've found? Duck Jesus is the only way. He will hear the call of the sincere, but shun those without faith. And we must have faith, brothers and sisters of Sugar Valley. We must.

"I want you to gather in a circle and pray with me. I want you to join hands as we put our fate in the palm of the Almighty. We will find that which we seek. But it shall not be through the violence of beheading, nor the chemical and shock treatments. Duck Jesus, please heed our call."

Courtney clasped hands with her husband, who was kneeling by the side of Father Mallardy. She was grateful for the pastor's compassionate wisdom, although his rhetoric struck her as extreme and somewhat random.

"No, a thousand times no, to the beheading," said Mallardy. "But these memories must be dealt with. And if the children…" Fat tears rolled down his cheeks as he uttered these words. "I'm sorry…if the children find out what the fathers and the mothers have been doing in their name, their bitter legacy…perhaps…yes, it's coming to me now. Perhaps we shall have to call upon the dark side. I hear Duck Jesus talkin' to me now, in my good ear, and he's sayin,'—blessed be his name—he's sayin,' use the fallen woman, the Jezebel, this Dr. Flesh, whose evil has contrived the blasphemy of the Reality Stack. Through her erotic torture devices, she will convert these memories that are surgin' up and makin' of our mothers and sisters and daughters a hot mess thereof, change the current…"

"So that's a definite 'no' to the beheadings?" asked Courtney, her voice tremulous.

"Forces are in motion," said Mallardy. "And Duck Jesus, for reasons known only to himself, has decreed that some shall indeed perish in that awful way. But for the rest, the other path shall be trod. That of the electrodes and the clamps and the bindin.'"

Courtney observed, but quickly pushed out of her mind, that Mallardy's trousers stretched a bit further when he spoke of Dr. Flesh, and she wondered if anyone else saw. She hoped there was a method to his very apparent madness, but aside from that, vowed to herself to patiently obey the will of the patriarchs of Sugar Valley, who kept her in bling and snuff boxes packed with the wicked candy.

***

Victoria D'Allessandro closed the outer office door gingerly, feeling in her purse to reassure herself that scripts were indeed present. She could still taste Fassbinder's ancient Teutonic pussy on her tongue, with all its accents of the Black Forest and revels in lederhosen. In the corridor, a hunchbacked figure waited, tracking Victoria as she exited the building by the back steps and walked towards her Jaguar, parked in the main lot of the industrial park.

By the time she became aware of her assassin, the axe had already whistled halfway through its arc, cleaving off her head, which rolled across the tarmac to be followed by her body and her purse. The prescription fell out of the purse along with a roll of condoms, a hairbrush and a nail file, lifted by a sudden, strong gust of wind and carried away by a cartoon-like crow that seemed to emit its own weather system as it flew.

***

"Oh come on now," said Sweetback Glade. "I thought all those years in homicide made you hardcore. You're acting like a green rookie."

He stepped aside to avoid getting vomit on his Italian dress shoes. His partner, Joe Oroborus, continued to retch until nothing came out but gasps and sobs.

"You mean to tell me you never saw a headless body before?"

Oroborus covered his mouth with one hand and raised an arm. Green juice trickled down his sleeves.

"Fuck's sake," said Glade. "When we report this to the cops, we can't be sick and dying and shit. That's this girl's job." He nudged the corpse with a stick. "Right? And there ain't even any fresh blood. It's just that brown gunk."

Oroborus finally found his voice. "I was never in homicide. I was an undercover vice cop."

"You mean…"

"Yeah, all that time I was assigned to track you. Your movements, your shenanigans and escapades."

Glide slapped his own face with a broad pink palm. "There's such a thing as trust. So I trusted a lying, duplicitous motherfucker to cover my ass, and all along you were reporting on me? Good thing I kept my service revolver. I've got half a mind to let you join Headless Nelly over here."

❄❄❄

Eighteen Years Previous

"We're ready for you, Mr. Shreck, any time."

Shreck dangled the megaphone between his legs. What to say this time that hadn't already been said.

This was not a movie anymore. It was corpses—piles of them, eyes fixed in horror at the last moment, caught blind in the throes of orgasm, axed in the trembling instant that flesh poured out like a muddy stream, the pure, sparkling bliss of its release fixed permanently on celluloid.

There were so many, where they came from even Shreck didn't know. The past week had swept through like a hurricane, teeming with bright-eyed starlets brought forth on their knees to taste the glory of video stardom, only to be shredded, beheaded, drilled, sucked to screaming dust.

At first the operation had proceeded smoothly. Shreck understood what was needed, had rendered the blueprints with mathematical exactitude. The models he had made—of clay, of Styrofoam, of hair gel, of carpet garf—stood silently in the warehouse, templates of perfection. The goal, the vision, might take years to come to fruition: a race of flawless blondes, able to shop without fatigue, wear the clothes created for them, eat the foods designed for them, think the thoughts constructed for them, and when the time came, vote for the candidate with their best interests at heart.

It all looked good on paper, or modeling clay, or foam blobs angrily melted together. But the reality was so very different. Shreck had practically broken down and cried at the feet of the mannequin, its head perforated and leaking with gokkun, its perfect blondeness evident even in its ankles, its toes, the wonderful arches of its feet.

If it were only warm flesh, a real surf god; if, like some latter-day Pygmalion, the love he'd poured out before it, and onto it, the love he'd squeezed from a lifetime of longing and splashed on its six-pack, its smooth and unformed genitals, could bring the creature to life. Without the wading in gore, the hacking into the night, the bellowing, the frenzied fugue states in which all body parts began to blur into one another, as though human was just another word for modular unit, and science just a beast with a throbbing stiffie.

But wishes wouldn't bring the creature to life. Relentless masturbation wouldn't animate it. First, it had to be conceived; then, the parts had to be found; then, assembled correctly, coldly, without ardor, according to the models and blueprints.

The passage from premise to fulfillment was fraught with bawling runaways and graphic close-ups, punched sockets brimming over with spunk, heads sutured together and then ripped apart in a spasmodic symphony of pain—all to find the exact configuration. The fit. Experimentation was a cruel business, even more so when the actors, plucked from the streets and alleyways of Horrorweird, had come to the city of dreams with stars in their eyes, hoping to become famous, smiling down from billboards, signing autographs on glossy prints, making themselves available to their many, many fans.

It was said that here everybody wanted a piece of you. Shreck knew the bone-hard reality of that.

But there was a time for contemplation and a time for action.

"Ready when you are, Mr. Shreck."

He picked up the megaphone. "Action," he said.

***

Shreck's creation was called Rocko Bentwood, after the man who had donated his brain. Rocko's brain, formerly the command and control center for the 39-year-old lead singer of the doom metal band Funeralopolis, contained intelligence adequate to the task of voicing dreary, Lovecraftian lyrics about the imminent clown apocalypse. However, that was not the trait Shreck had selected him for. Simply put, Rocko had a genius for pussy— mesmerizing its owners and luring them back to his trailer for a session of the old "Who's Your Father." Except that when the groupie of the moment discovered that the expected package was only a carrot stick, she most often bailed. That deficit had been filled by Mort Zorn of Citizens, Inc., the child guitar prodigy turned porn impresario turned suspension artist, whose meat had been hailed as "impressive...daunting" by one of the top actresses in adult film.

Rocko lost his head in a deadly game of "who can swallow the worst vomit," in which a bolus of sick was expelled directly into the gaping maw of the next party in a circle, who added their own toxic payload, until the final recipient received an emetic cocktail so powerful they either keeled over on the spot or lived, forever transformed, to tell the tale. In Rocko's case, he had actually chickened out at the point where the vomitus had begun to glow, fled into the night screaming and naked only to be instantly flattened—save for his brain—by a tanker truck that had jumped an embankment into a residential neighborhood of the Hollyweird Hills. At which point a sensor was activated, a team of masked pataphysicians was summoned, and the brain, still pulsing, was instantly frozen and delivered via bicycle messenger to Shreck's secret lab. Zorn, less fortunate in some respects and more in others, lived on sans sausage, wiser and sadder, having lost his erotic instrument in an act of retribution by the above-mentioned adult film actress.

The creature's massive, chiseled torso, chest and belly came involuntary courtesy of "Thunk" Thornsen, the Norwegian wrestling champ, whose intake of steroids made his head shrivel on his neck and one day simply vanish, leaving the body to fend for itself. The arms had belonged to Biff Baxter, drummer for the semi-legendary Bozokill, the rest of whom was currently in the hands of the clowns. Which left bassist Vern Gormenstein, who lost both legs and head in the surf off Osso Beach. And thus, a village of rivetheads raised a Frankenchild with the deft assistance of Dr. Shreck and the Burp Me Melmo puppet now known as Dr. Fuzzly, injected with a solution of free-form DNA and released among the barely legal senior girls of Sugar Valley High to propagate the True Blonde Cohort.

***

Present Day or Thereabouts

Halfway through her sophomore year at Sugar Valley High, the girl known sometimes as Ravyn Blackstone and otherwise as a pixelated sigil paused with her fingers over her laptop's keyboard, wondering how she had come to accumulate such bad social karma. The cafeteria was filled with the electric excitement that always preceded a home game and the Death Ball squad was engaged in a vigorous food fight, mashed potatoes sailing across the room, drumsticks wielded like clubs, soda squirted from high-pressure hoses, all with the tacit approval if not active encouragement of the school's administration. Blackstone thought longingly of her days at the progressive institution in Missoula and the vicious carnival that had replaced it.

She had very few friends, and even these were absent today, one girl recovering from cheerleader assault, another nursing wounds delivered in a role playing game gone wrong, and the fourth member of the Geek Squad, the only boy, having simply vanished.

Ravyn very much wished she were 30 instead of 16 and that her mother hadn't dragged her from Montana to California in the wake of mom's second marriage, this time to real estate god Henry Hornburger. Sugar Valley High wasn't simply a secondary school, it was an exclusive club that rejected people like Ravyn on principle. For one thing, she wasn't a size 4 blonde, had no aptitude for or interest in sports, buffed-out guys, hair products or small salads. She was proud of her curves and her long, curly gypsy-black hair, loved goth rock and heavy metal and went out of her way to distinguish herself from the other girls, sporting

Mayhem and Bad Religion T's, denim jackets with swatches of band patches, ripped jeans and Chuck Taylor's. And although she was very, very lonely, she kept herself in reasonably good spirits by writing down her thoughts, fantasies and schema for world conquest on her laptop. When she wasn't being pelted with French fries and showered with strawberry milkshakes.

She stood up, dripping grease, her face bright red.

"Can't take the heat, huh?" yelled the Captain of the Death Ball team, Bob Hufford. Ravyn tried her very best to ignore him, his obvious lechery disguised as harassment, his ripped stomach muscles and formidable biceps, his cruel, sensuous mouth. She closed her laptop, put it in her handbag, and carried her lunch tray over to the nearest trash bin. Hufford took this opportunity to get in her face.

"Hi," he said, his blond curls dancing over smooth, cover boy-handsome features. "You're not going to leave now, I hope."

Ravyn averted her gaze. She found him attractive in a guilty pleasures kind of way, but would sooner chew ground glass than in any way reciprocate his crude advances. Even though he was playing to the groundlings, mocking her, she instinctively recognized that he liked her too, if only at a basic, sexual level. She stayed quiet. Hufford had her wedged between a table full of insufferable small salad-eaters and the trash bin. There was no polite or inconspicuous way to escape him.

"Excuse me," she said, moving forward with determined steps in the direction of the exit, about five feet away from the end of the lunch counter. At the last second, the Captain stepped aside and let her pass, but not without smacking her butt, which brought a howl from his team-mates and derisive giggles from the small salad-eaters.

The cafeteria opened onto a hallway. With her head down, Ravyn walked past the utility room, the Drama Club office and an old, dust-laden trophy case from the pre-Death Ball era, turned right and fished in her jeans pocket for the key to the AV Room. She had work to do, and refused to be disturbed from it a moment longer.

Inside the AV Room, glorious quiet. Ravyn set down her handbag on a long aluminum table, drew up a chair and retrieved the laptop. Her mind was brimming with a story idea that had come to her the week before, when she'd been visiting a friend in Horrorweird. She and her friend had been window-shopping when Ravyn saw a girl of about her own age sitting on a bus bench, a distracted look on her face. The girl was a short, plump Latina with big, startlingly beautiful eyes that seemed to hold tragedy in them. She was sipping from a plastic thermos and tapping her scuffed sneakers to some internal music. Watching her, Ravyn felt a sudden surge of empathy for the girl. It was almost as though the dark eyes were relaying a story to her and if she concentrated she could take it down by psychic dictation. Then the bus came and the girl was swallowed up and carried away.

Ravyn bent to her task. "Paying no heed to the incoherent demands of the mother-mass plumped deep in an armchair that dominated her living room like a thrift store throne," she typed, "Samantha Gomez ran straight to her bedroom, locked the door and hurled her body down on the pink comforter. Her shoulders rose and fell as she sobbed."

A sudden surge of noisy movement came from the hallway as the cafeteria disgorged its contents. The buzzer rang shrilly, followed by a stampede as the students rushed to their next classes. Distracted, she looked up from the screen. With the disturbance, her story had vanished to some now irretrievable middle distance, and Ravyn thought hoped it might return if she focused on something else. Something random.

Behind the table were four steel filing cabinets that glinted with the light from a horizontal window high on the wall that looked out over the Death Ball field. Ravyn closed her laptop, got up and began opening drawers in the first filing cabinet with no particular goal. It was filled with plastic binders full of photographs of school celebrities past. Sliding that cabinet closed, she decided on a random instinct to check the top one. At first it stuck, then suddenly shrieked open as a VHS cassette tumbled from the top of a stack and fell to the floor.

Ravyn bent down and picked up the cassette. The white label was marked with a single word: "Shreck."

***

After twenty minutes of viewing the tape, Ravyn shut her eyes and folded her arms around her stomach. She didn't want to pass out, not quite yet at least, although from the way her guts were jumping around, sweet oblivion wasn't on the menu. She had thrown up in her mouth, more than a little, from the relentless battery of violent and disgusting images, redolent of the Cowin necroslushy aesthetic at its most advanced stage of decay.

Whoever was responsible for the cinematic spew recorded on different types of film stock, HD video and other sources deserved the strappado, for starters, followed by boiling in oil and other medieval torture forms. Which didn't quite account for the surge of pleasure that went immediately to her groin once she'd overcome the initial nausea, and the panty-soaking that followed shortly thereafter.

The TV set she was using as a monitor seemed almost infected by the rank tableau that had crossed it; there was an unusual sheen over the screen that she'd never seen before, and even after she had stopped the tape, some of the images remained, as though their evil was so intense it had simply burned itself in.

***

"Well, that was curious," said Paul Diamond, the sole male member of the Geek Squad. He wiped his forehead with a pale yellow napkin, the rolls of fat trembling beneath his Extra Large Dr. Who Vs. the Daleks t-shirt. The Squad was assembled in the basement of Blackstone's house in East Sugar Valley, Diamond sitting cross-legged on the floor.

"What do you think?" asked Ravyn, who was sitting on the couch opposite to Diamond along with the two girls.

"I think it's horrible!" burst out Alice O'Halloran, she of the orange-red hair, ultra-pale skin and freckles. Then she was silent, her thin shoulders moving up and down spasmodically as she quietly wept.

"I don't know," threw in Mintzy Spielbaum, who most closely resembled Ravyn in size, stature and coloration. "There were moments I thought I was going to vomit, but then again, there's something almost...ok, you're going to think I'm a total perv, but, there's something kind of hot about the tape. Especially all that girl on girl action." She suddenly colored, realizing what she had just said.

"I don't remember any girl on girl action," said Ravyn.

"Oh yeah, well there was a little burst of it towards the end," said Mintzy. "A trace. Almost subliminal. Ok, maybe I just projected it."

"It's perfectly normal to have those desires," said Paul kindly. "It doesn't make you a bad person."

Ravyn threw up her arms. "Right, so, before this degenerates into a group confessional, I really want to know what

- 102 -

you guys think about the tape, and what's on it, and what we should do about it, if anything."

"All right," said Paul. "I think what we're looking at is an experiment of some kind. Or an attempt to make monster porn. But the realism of it...that's what gets me. And you almost recognize some of the girls, right? They look like our classmates. The others. The blondes."

The other three nodded in unison. "Ok, I'm just throwing this out there," said Mintzy. "But maybe, maybe there's a connection. To our classmates, I mean. When do you think the tape was made?"

"That's easy," said Paul. "There's a timestamp at the bottom. December 1994."

"Eighteen years ago," said Mintzy.

"Right, right," said Ravyn. "So if we put it all together, eighteen years ago, there was this experiment, and it was recorded...an experiment that involved, um, wait, the blondes' moms. Some crazy shit. A heavy metal Frankenstein monster, a fucking...mad scientist with a puppet glued on his hand, hardcore penetration, more jizz than I'm frankly comfortable with, and...maybe a little girl on girl action at the end."

Mintzy smiled and nodded enthusiastically.

"And it was just lying there in the cabinet waiting for you to discover it," said Paul. "That's just fishy. First of all, it's evidence of a crime. A few of the girls look underage, they've obviously been coerced, maybe drugged, kidnapped and raped by the creature while the whole thing is being filmed. It's not the kind of thing you just find in the AV room. Someone put it there. The question is, who, and why?"

"I dunno," said Ravyn. "Or...maybe I do. It has to be Ms. Bunford. She gave me a copy of the key to the room. She's always been, I guess sympathetic is the right word. Like she gets us, gets the whole Geek Squad thing. I've never seen her hanging out with any of the other teachers, except when there's faculty meetings. She doesn't car pool, she doesn't socialize, she just does her own thing. Like we do. But…oh hell, why don't we just give her a call?"

"I agree," said Paul. "Either it's her and she can fill us in, or it isn't, and, well, maybe we all got loaded on cough syrup or something, and it's awkward, but Ms. Bunford seems like the kind of lady who's been there, you know what I mean?"

***

"I'm so happy to see you all here," said Linnea Bunford to the Geek Squad, cozily settled around her couch in the little cottage she owned near the woods, right before the freeway to Bone City. "Having to keep a secret all these years, well, it became too much for me. I had to share. I knew I could trust you with the information, because it's critical you understand what happened nearly twenty years ago, and what's happening to our community now. The future—if there is to be such a thing—rests on your tender but very capable shoulders.

"Like you, I was never a joiner. There were reasons for that, maybe personal, maybe not. I moved to Sugar Valley forty years ago with my husband, now deceased, God rest his soul. Mr. Bunford was a gentleman, a courageous and outspoken advocate of ideas that are now fairly mainstream, but at the time were considered heresy, especially here. They only tolerated him because of his immense wealth, and then barely. As for me, I was the wife— a liberal, a radical, political. Which made me poison to them. But I didn't care. I never really cared. I was happy to be the school librarian, which put me in a position where I could encourage students who were different as I was, as I am. Point them in the right direction. Guide them.

"We're at a tipping point as a nation, as a culture. What's going on in Sugar Valley is just a reflection of that, a microcosm of larger forces. The old guard still wants to preserve their hallucination of a pure bloodline, whatever that is. But what they didn't get, and will never appreciate, is the insanity of wanting that purity. Unmixed, they think, therefore untainted. But you can't stop evolution. There's only one way, and it's forward. Oh, listen to me rattle on. It's not so important what I say, or even what happens to me after this. But you young people...I'm sorry, I can't talk right now."

"That's totally cool," said Ravyn. "We just appreciate that you trust us. But what do you want us to do? What can we do? We're just kids."

Ms. Bunford took a deep breath. "I'd like you to meet a dear old friend of mine. He will help explain. Oh Fuzzly!"

They turned around as a familiar figure walked into the room. He was furry and red and his eyes rolled freely in their plastic cornea.

"B-Burp Me Melmo?" gasped Mintzy.

Dr. Fuzzly settled into a lounge chair near the fireplace, a thoughtful expression on his face. He slowly packed his pipe, torched the kindness with a wooden match and inhaled. "It's good to see all of you here," he said after awhile. "Children of this generation...meh. But you know all about that now."

"You escaped from the clutches of that evil Shreck!" Alice said suddenly.

"We escaped...from one another. Ours was a symbiotic, deeply complex relationship," said Fuzzly. We worked together until we were forced apart. After that came the deluge. I was a wanted butt-puppet, sought by the federal government for trumped-up crimes. They looked for me everywhere, but I hid. Sometimes in plain sight, for example that one reality show—

Whatever Happened to Burp Me Melmo? Of course we made up some bullshit for the viewers. Said I had a hardcore Tide addiction, disappeared into the Hondurican jungle and joined this revolutionary circus. That part was halfway true, actually. I've been through so much since Shreck and I...anyway. Ancient history. You might say I'm a reformed puppet. I've changed, see. Shreck used me for his evil plans, but you know what, I can't say I blame him either. We were all conscripted, some of us grafted on to hands, others...other places. I was lucky. After awhile you stop struggling and learn to enjoy it. Adopt or die. Well, I'm old now, but there's still a chance for you lot. Only you have to get out of here, and I mean now. Don't wait. Don't wait till the duck priest finds out about you. Stay one step...ahead of them. They will turn clown, oh yes. I saw what happened to Shreck's prototypes. Even now there are days I wake up in a cold sweat to the sound of bicycle horns."

Tears welled in his saucer-like eyes. Ms. Bunford reached down, picked up the puppet and sat him in her lap.

"I've suffered...oh, how I have suffered," he said, sniffling.

"There, there."

Fuzzly let out a long, loud burp, and Bunford patted him gently on the belly.

IV.

Bone City, 1994

Shreck pressed a button on the control panel. The centrifuge whirled again.

Fuck if he knew went into the mix this time. It had been a long and complicated night.

Tinkering with the human genome was a sideline. Shreck's heart lay in videos now—directing when he could, but also cinematography and sometimes choreography if dance was involved. But he had undertaken this chore—this bitter, godawful assignment—and he would see it through to the end. Even if many had to die in the process.

The body count was ridiculous. Who knew there'd be so much waste involved, so many buckets slopping with organs that would never see use, besides the usual eyeball boxes—like Joseph Cornell on the corpse juice—and whimsical arrangements of stiffs. The Sugar Valley crowd never really saw the point of these, as hard as he tried to convince them that he needed to let off steam. Sometimes that meant digging around in a cheerleader's guts, stripping off his sterile nitrile gloves so he could *get right in there*, preserving her screams for use in an ongoing industrial noise project, and for the following weeks noting the stages of de/composition, the rank, sugary smell as the body grew rigid, then wet, finally achieving its apotheosis as acid-eaten bone. Where its resurrection as sculpture began.

He looked up at the monitors. They scrawled the usual peptide chains and polymerase combinations, gabba gabba hey, we accept her, etc. He'd thrown in some salamander this time, the Hamburger Helper of rogue genetic science, hoping to see some improvement in the prototype.

The pink sludge had begun to form at the base of the cylinder. Slowly taking shape as the ultimate doll, the perfect playmate. The apogee of blondeness.

Shreck's heart skipped a beat. He punched some random numbers into the sequence, ran his fingers through his hair, took a swallow from the mason jar and made a wry face. It had been a long but productive night, from the taste of it.

He realized he had no business manning this particular ship. As a latter-day Frankenstein toiling in his underground laboratory to create the ideal mall-walker, he suspected his true talents lay elsewhere. Nevertheless, he would be damned if he didn't finish the job. Even if it took blood, sweat, tears, horrible nightmares, tyranny, mutations that had to be quickly put down, and baroque variations on the double-helix model that left wiser heads securely planted over his notebooks and re-utilized as lamps.

Was it soup? Was it the real turtle dove, or only the rock lobster? He fanned himself. The lab was getting stuffy.

And the pink pulp was forming limbs. The girl looked like rubber, but with such a wonderful texture. He couldn't wait till she had fully formed in the cylinder to waltz her around the lab, even if her head fell off and had to be sutured onto another body, as happened nine times out of ten.

He looked up the monitor. The sequence was slowing down. Another trickle of bases, a little glee-dance for good luck, a quick snort of the fun powder, and…nothing.

Still, 80% of a successful experiment was something more than his competitors had accomplished. Did he have any competitors? Or, as he most feared, was he operating solo—the playing field his and his alone, the protocols cooked in hell, the very nature of his experiments condemned by wisdom, common sense and the strict limits of sanity?

Not that it mattered. At the end of the day, he got the check. And if he was lucky, a discount on hermaphrodite whores.

Shreck just wanted to play rock and roll. Lou Reed during his *Transformer* period, preferably, or Bowie's Thin White Duke, throwing darts in lover's eyes. He knew fuck all about making workable fleshbots. But the money was far too good to pass up. And he was so close to a solution now, he could feel it thrumming in his blood.

There came a gurgling sound from the cylinder. The centrifuge had started again, on its own. Dripping strands into the helical matrix, a little dab'll do ya, *et voila*—this time, the soup.

The cylinder opened, and the girl opened its eyes.

She was the ideal, pink in every way, blonde where it counted, a blank void yawning behind her baby blues.

"It's...not dead!" exulted Shreck, taking the girl's hands and whirling her about the lab.

Her eyelashes had just begun to sprout, right on time for batting practice. "Hello there," said Shreck, looking deep into her eyes. "How does it feel to be newly arrived?"

"I feel like...shopping," said the girl, tossing her head until the blonde curls showered down her back. "I feel like...buying...stuff."

"Excellent," said Shreck. "I love it. Anything else?"

"I'm so...hot."

"Yes you are, my pretty girl, yes you are."

Shreck's Journal

So I get this call from Hank Owens, a friend of mine who lives on the hill—Sugar Valley. A real doctor, from what I can remember, although those days are obscured by clouds. We did a lot of solvents in college, hazed and were hazed, sometimes both at once. A lot of trauma, self-inflicted and the other kind. But that's history. The important thing was that I had a job. I was making these videos for a glam metal band called FuckAngel, half-assed artsy shit. The lead singer was living with his girlfriend, who supported him on her salary as a paid intern for Wanton Meat, Inc. They weren't exactly loaded, but they had the kind of green you don't see much of these days, especially in the circles I come from. And boy, are those circles—wheels within wheels. I had a pentagram half chalked in when the phone call came. I said hello, hoping there was money on the other end. And sure enough, I felt that green buzz. You know the kind. No, not that. Why am I addressing a ghost reader? Anyway, he told me to get my ass out to the hill because there were some people who wanted to talk with me. They required my special talents, such as they are.

Okay, I said. I had nothing to wear. At least nothing that would impress the hill people that I was qualified to do more than wash their cars or rape their nubile daughters. Just the thought gave me wood. I rubbed out the chalk with my sock toe and checked the closet. My wardrobe in those days was halfway between Liberace and punk rock—a lot of shredded suits with mirrors on them. A pile of curdled jeans. Some underwear that had seen better days. Some underwear that looked like I could resuscitate it, at least better than the girl at the club. Boy, was that a toilet case! I could still smell her baby whore perfume.

But to business. I found one clean dress shirt—violet, it so happened, which suited my needs. Best to look queer, especially with these folks. And one half of a suit, charcoal gray slacks. They kind of matched if you squinted. I finished up the outfit with a gray jacket, slightly crumpled, and a burgundy tie. I checked myself out in the bathroom mirror. Not half bad. Then I remembered the lipstick. It was a dark red "fuck me" color. Glad I caught that in time! I rubbed it off with some cotton balls that I was pretty sure didn't have any solvents in them, called a taxi and waited.

It took the guy two hours of getting me lost on narrow, winding streets for him to charge me 60 bucks. I tried to argue with him but he threw a fit in some Slavic language, so I peeled off some counterfeit bills—no need to argue in a language I didn't understand—and stepped out into the street.

There was pin-drop silence. Immaculate green lawns. I felt like I was polluting their precious air just using it to breathe. The address was this mansion, gravel pathway, huge garage, at least three entrances that I could detect. I went up to what looked like the main door and pressed the buzzer. Nothing. Then my friend came to the door. I was so relieved I nearly shit myself. He took me to a living room where these middle-aged white women were sipping coffee and talking loudly about appliances. They took one look at me and I could tell they were skeptical. At least I wasn't wearing a mask, I thought.

A man came into the room. He was sweating heavily, overweight, apologetic. He asked me if I wanted anything to drink. I said I was fine—which was true because I'd done a little X to gird myself. It was starting to kick in now and I felt friendlier than I usually did. The man was an old Death Ball star, I recognized him from the funny papers.

So this was the gig: they wanted me to make them the perfect blonde, blondes, a whole army of them. They were determined that the following generation would respect their traditions. They were concerned about the influx of rap and hip-hop into their blonde community and some of the weirder races their daughters had been associated with. Their conversation was peppered with references to Death Ball and Jesus and how good Jesus's butt had looked in those tight, tight DB pants.

I was a little appalled—this was coming from the guy, I mean all that stuff about Jesus ass. But I kept quiet.

It seemed pointless to explain to these people that my knowledge of genetics ended with sophomore biology in high school and that I'd spent most of the class drawing elaborate pornographic space operas modeled after the stories in *Heavy Metal* magazine. I vaguely recalled something about an Austrian monk named Gregor Mendel and his hybrids. Then there were some other guys, Watson and Holmes, and they came up with the model for DNA. Watson was big into opium, from what I remembered, and Holmes was a spastic with a preference for dwarf amputees. I pretended to listen but figured I would do as I usually did, look a few things up on the Internet and fill in the rest from my jaded imagination. It was a good hook, though. Other than some obvious legal angles, the prospect of making a nice, big-assed blonde girl in a lab just tickled my fancy. And with these guys throwing me the long green, I really couldn't lose.

***

Now, Roughly Speaking

The private detective agency of Oroborus and Glide was on a stakeout in Sugar Valley. Strange things had been happening with the students and faculty of the elite high school, but the detectives were there for another purpose. To whit, watching the house of an SV society lady who might, according to their source, be using it as a wetback brothel.

They had the wrong house, but it didn't matter because they had confused the case with another one. This happened frequently.

"I do not believe this shit," said Sweetback Glide, stretching the newspaper over his knee. Even after three days and nights of the stakeout, he looked great—6 feet 2 inches of solid muscle packed tightly in a glove of chocolate skin.

Joe Oroborus, who was only 5 feet, felt cramped in the surveillance van. "What's up, Sweet?"

"Well, check this out. Says here—and it's a long-ass read, but it's good—scientists in Italy discovered this new strain of DNA, it's called free-form. Bonds to anything, something dies it picks it right up, you can glue things together that were never meant to be. Like some Superglue shit, only genetic. Now if I could only get me some of that, swap some of my old girlfriends around, know what I'm saying? Take this one's pussy and that one's mouth and this one's fine long hair, take a chunk of the other one's attitude and toss it in the trash, you know. I'm gonna build me a woman. That's the way. You gotta use science these days, Joe. Look out honey, I'm using technology, you know? That's the answer. It's the key."

"Sounds fascinating," said Oroborus. He yawned. "Hey, do you have any of that heroin left over from last night?"

"Heroin? Are you crazy in the magic now? Yes, you white, you crazy all right, but *are you crazy?* I ask this again because the last time you did that shit, you nodded off right in the middle of an interrogation. We had that son of a bitch dead to rights. He was gonna crack. Then all of a sudden Mr. Honkey here takes a nap. A goddam nap! Little fool was smuggling jewelry up his ass in a finger-stall and selling it to the Mexican Mafia for that high-class pussysmoke."

"I don't remember anything about that," said Oroborus. "C'mon, please? Just a smidge. My back hurts like hell. We've been cramped up in this van for hours and I don't think he's coming out. Couldn't we just set up the robot and get back to the bar for shots or something?"

"Now I see how it is," said Glide

"How what is?"

"How the worm turns. Now back when we was real detectives, or as you say, soft detectives—but we were real detectives, had us some serious badges —you kept whining about how we was gonna solve ourselves some cases and follow leads instead of just hanging out on my stoop and drinking malt liquor. Now we citizens—okay, barely legal, but we citizens—you do a complete 180, some Linda Blair shit. Hell man, you ain't done nothing since we started this business but sit on your ass and imagine all the work you're *gonna* do when you get motivated.

"Meanwhile, I do all the leg-work. I gotta sleep with all them white women. I gotta use my gat on occasion or break a man's spirit down just in case he wants to pull some state's evidence bullshit. Turn us in, when we the detectives. Thinks he's gonna bring the hard pussy. Oh yeah, for a soft detective you were real tough, man, real tough. Back in the day. Now you can barely sit up."

"Yeah, I know. But I'm telling you, we're wasting our time. We should use the robot. Hey, you're always saying we need to upgrade our technology. Well, here's a chance. We haven't used the 'bot since the Mystery Drink Caper back in '05."

"Uh-huh. And that worked out real good. That 'bot was stewing in shit for an entire weekend, I mean marinating. Stunk so bad we had to dissolve the little bitch in acid and start right over from the black box. Frightening, the smells. 'Cause it wasn't just no ass-rind either, something else got added to the mix. Spicy, complex as the barrel of a nanogun, but hell on the sinuses."

"Right, but the new 'bot is better than ever, and besides, I wanna do some shots."

"The man wants to get his drink on."

"Yuppers."

"And he wants some of that China White."

"Double yuppers."

"And he ain't got 'I'm a crazy white man' written on his forehead in invisible ink."

"Nope."

"Well okay. Can't tell anyway, 'cause I ain't got my 'crazy white man' scanner with me at the moment. I've got a little bit of the horse left, enough for both of us. We're gonna have to cold shake the motherfucker 'cause ain't no water in here. Another little something a certain someone forgot because he was too damn high to worry about the details of his next too damn high...never mind."

Ten Minutes Later

"Now what was all this about free-form DNA?"

"You know, you curious. Usually you don't pay attention to nothin' I say, all of a sudden you all about the DNA and shit. Why?"

"You don't have to be an asshole about it. I'm not a suspect. We're not down in the hole with electrodes and gore candy, got some citizen plugged up his ass with insects..."

"Yeah, sorry about that. Well, free-form DNA will do a man right. Ain't got a date for a Saturday night, shit, he goes down to the city morgue, they got some fine-ass white girls in there, pull 'em off the slab, dump 'em in a bag, take them down to that little lab we got going in East SoNoe and start the refinements, as I call them."

"We have a *lab?*"

"Not yet. But I'm working on it. Now shut up. I found something else too. There was a man right here in town, I mean smack dab in the middle of this fake plastic studio environment, they called him Dr. Shreck. Turns out he was some video director or some shit, made a bunch of crappy videos of glam metal bands, but check it out—that wasn't his only gig. He called himself 'Doctor' but he was a Doctor of Theology. Yeah, that's right. Went to some Christian school in the Midwest. Had no business rooting around in cadavers and extracting the pink flavah, you know?"

"Maybe...it's just me...but half the time I have no idea what you're going on about, Sweet."

"Maybe...it's just me...but half the time I just want to kick your ass and not bother with the reasoning behind it."

"Maybe...we're just incompatible."

"Now you hurtin' my feelings."

"I thought you had a heart of steel?"

"I was just joking about that shit. Ok, so I do have a heart of steel. But my real heart, or, damn, how should I phrase it, my poetic heart is solid. I'm deep. Unlike some white trash no soul wannabe private dicks of my unfortunate acquaintance."

"Okay, cut the crap. Do you think there's a connection between those two articles?"

"Hell yes there's a connection. They were both written by the same guy. Look, this dude. Roland Hymsaw. What kind of name is that?"

"We're going to pay Hymsaw a little visit."

"Okay, now you're frightening me."

"But it's the only way."

Oroborus twisted the key in the ignition. "You're right, Sweet. It's the only way."

"White boy got some sense in him after all," mumbled Glide.

**

"I don't want any trouble, guys," said Roland Hymsaw. He was dressed in baggy shorts and a ripped Slayer t-shirt with a bathrobe over them. His ass-length hair was dyed a luminous green. He gestured to an overstuffed sofa.

"Trouble? I don't see no trouble. Do you see trouble?"

"Cut the crap, Glide. Hey, seriously, my partner here is just a little wired right now. But you've got the medicine. Right?"

"I have no idea what this white motherfucker is talking about. Can we come in?"

"Sure, guys. Sorry, I'm still waking up. Long night."

"So what can you tell us about this Shreck dude?"

"My partner thinks there's a connection…"

Glide put up a hand. "Not yet. What's your angle?"

"Have a seat. Shreck's been around for a long time. He's kind of a fixture on the Horrorweird scene, always has some kind of project going on, but nothing solid. It all depends on who you talk to. I interviewed one girl who thinks he's a flat-out genius. Seriously misunderstood. Now her knowledge of Shreck was limited to heavy metal videos, and specifically, hair products. She does metal hair. I think she was impressed by the lighting in the one video he did for Fuckangel. Then she disappeared. Phone disconnected, no way to contact her. Then I get this call from a guy—maybe it was a girl, it was kind of hard to tell, but they had a really strange, low voice. Said Shreck was running an illegal lab and doing all kinds of heinous experiments. I followed him one time to this address in Sugar Valley..."

"Really," said Glide. He gave Oroborus a significant look. "What would a low-rent operator like Shreck be doing in Sugar Valley?"

"I have no idea. But I'm pretty sure it's connected to the lab."

"Where is this lab now?"

"He's using a warehouse in Bone City, right on the outskirts. Sketchy part of town. Doing some kind of Viola Flesh number..."

"Wait, did you say Viola Flesh?"

"You know her?"

"Only by reputation. I like some of her movies. That *Reality Stack* was fine. You know the one, Joe, where the movie kind of ingests your brain. Fucks you up for months afterwards, like a bad acid trip, but I really got a kick out of it. Went to this Caribbean island and got my dick torn out by witches. Then this shark fucked me in the ass. But it changes...last I heard the witches and shark-fucking got replaced by something even stranger, like some monkey brains, melon on stilts shit. You know how it goes."

"Yeah," said Hymsaw. "That's the one."

Back in the Dizzel, Fo Shiz

The mutiny had been building for weeks now. Shreck's right hand, possessed and dominated by the Burp Me Melmo puppet now known as Dr. Fuzzly, had its own will and agenda. He would wake up to find himself menaced by the puppet, inches from his face, sputtering threats and demands. Shreck no longer had control over his hand, was helpless to counter the attacks that came at all hours now, fueled by Fuzzly's rage and resentment.

Arguing with the puppet was useless. Fuzzly felt he was owed equal control and say in all of Shreck's endeavors. But this was impossible for Shreck to grant. Operation True Blonde had powerful backers, moneyed interests with little use for the temper tantrums of a hand puppet with pretensions. When agents of the backers visited Shreck's studio/lab, he was hard-pressed to explain that Fuzzly's presence was purely accidental. At best, it seemed careless of Shreck, the fault of his unorthodox working style; at worst, a wild card that threatened to derail the project itself. It was only a matter of time before something radical would have to be done.

Shreck arose one morning with the puppet clamped onto his face like a limpet mine. He rolled straight out of bed, landing with the full force and weight of his body on the erstwhile Burp Me Melmo, who squeaked and moaned but held on like cold death. Shreck continued to roll, out of his bedroom and into the laboratory, the red fur full in his face, the little hairs bristling in his nose.

"This ends now!" Shreck rose to his feet and, half-blind, let his fingers do the walking through his instruments case, selecting a bone saw. He raised the saw with his left arm, powered it up and brought it down hard on his right wrist. The pain was enormous, but he cut until the puppet hand was completely severed.

Dr. Fuzzly yowled from the floor. "You can't do this to me! To us! We have a complicated, symbiotic relationship! There's still hope for us, isn't there? Don't you care? Did you ever care?"

Shreck was losing blood rapidly, but he still had the presence of mind to wrap a length of rubber surgical tubing around his arm as a rough tourniquet before hitting the panic button for the Naughty Nurse. Then he passed out, joining his former partner on the floor. The nurse found them in a tangled mass that reminded her of a baby and its mother. Only she couldn't quite tell who was who.

***

"Looking a little grey there, my man." Mike Volt swabbed the bar and started collecting the really gross glasses for the dishwasher.

"You have no idea," said Bramley Shomes, his hands shaking. "Pour me another, and keep 'em coming. I have a powerful   thirst   on   me."

"Maybe you should go home and sleep it off."

"Fat chance of that. I've seen things...they're scorched into my brain permanently, I think...has that ever happened to you?"

"Sure, there was this one time I was out in the woods back in Portland and this 50-foot gummy bear with eyes of fire tried to penetrate me. Sexually, I mean."

Bramley started. The reference to Portland and predatory gummy bears had awakened something buried deep in his subconscious. But that was not it. Not by a long shot.

"Drink your drink slowly this time," said Mike. "Don't just pound it down. I want to hear your story."

"I was doing security, you know, just the usual patrolling the strip mall and eating donuts, when we saw this strange light flickering from one of the houses right off 666 Street and Buʘuel. You know, the really random part. Shit, man, you see lights and then you see strange lights, you know? This one was strobing on and off. My partner was deep into some kind of glazed confection and couldn't be bothered, but I was bored as shit and needed action. Only so many times you can strip-search the homeless, and them smelling so *nasty*."

"Understood," said Mike. "Now drink your drink."

"I got a script,' said Vince. "This croaker gave it to me 'cause I complained of headaches...I don't even know what this shit is, but I got the script filled at the pharmacy."

Barmely pulled a crumpled white paper bag from his optical yellow security jacket and tore it open on the bar. "Yeah, ok, so I tell my partner I'm going to check it out. Strictly speaking, we're supposed to leave that kind of thing to the real cops, but I was craving adventure. My partner starts to nod off right into his donuts. I get the car and park it on a side street, then creep up through this alleyway and there's this fenced-in lawn that's just mutating with all kinds of weird plants I never seen before. It was spooky. Like Haunted Mansion spooky."

"Yeah, yeah. I've been down that road before."

"So you understand what I mean. I got out my flashlight and played it around the yard. Suddenly I saw these eyes staring back at me, they looked like they were on fire. Deep red, you know, the kind that haunt your dreams. It wasn't a dog or any kind of regular pet, it was like some kind of...like a lab experiment gone wrong. There were several sections, and part of it was like a worm and part of it was a hamster and then...it had these tits, I mean regular human girl tits. Then the thing started whimpering. I felt so sorry for it, but also like I had to get the hell out of there before I stumbled over anything else. The creature started making these horrible groaning noises, like rusty robot sex, and that set off an alarm. This cage came crashing down on me. I was totally trapped."

"Trapped in there with a chimerical type creature?"

"No, man, the thing set off the alarm with its noise, and then I was trapped in the cage alone. I waited there…I don't know how long. I had to pee so bad, finally I just unzipped. Fuck it, you know? Thought maybe if some sex pervert captured me to bukkake and slow roast I wasn't going in there with a full bladder."

VI.

The Creepy Origins of the Pink Holocaust

"Honey, we're going to have to do something."

"I agree, Von. But what?"

"It may be too late to help our princess, but now I'm thinking of the next generation. I've seen some of the girls Taffy has been hanging out with after school, and they're a bad bunch. What's worse, they all come from the same…the same *stock* as Taffy. Good blond stock. The same quality soup that gave us so many legends—like Cousin Biff, who still dominates the Death Ball squad. In the great beyond. I'm sorry, honey, I get so emotional."

"It's an emotional subject, dear."

"And then I think of Jesus."

"Oh dear," said Yvonne. "Must you?"

Von Gooch looked up, and for the first time saw doubt in his wife's eyes. The plague was spreading, the one he read about in his own personal copy of *The Holy Bible*, which he had pasted together one awful stormy night in a fugue state. He dimly remembered something about his meds and his wife's concern, but he was the one with vision. She couldn't see it, not yet. And now the plague had spread to their daughter, Taffitha, who they had raised to be the perfect blonde princess. Something had gone wrong, very, very wrong. The evil had infected his wife now. What was next?

He went on his knees and implored, "Please, Jesus, though we live in fallen times, and all are bedazzled by the charms of darkness, yet we might see a deeper, more penetrating light scouring through the pollution that is soiling our young people, our daughters and wives—the womenfolk."

"Von, maybe you should lie down. You look a little flushed. I'll get the thermometer. Remember what Dr. Owens said about your blood pressure."

"I know perfectly well what you mean by 'blood pressure,' dear. You mean that my prophetic tongue hath spouted words ye cannot grasp. Yet I assure ye that when the day of judgment comes, I will find myself on the right hand of the Almighty, and all who have doubted will be cast into the lake of Eternal Fire, there to turn like rotisserie chicken until the end of time."

"Which reminds me, honey, what did you want for dinner?"

"Dammit, woman, you're not listening to me."

"I'm sorry, honeycakes. I do try. Help me to understand." Yvonne made a mental note to call Dr. Owens and get a referral.

"It begins with liberal softening and it ends in drool and incontinence and fornication, my dear wife. It begins with some so-called 'hip-hop' music and it ends in heroin, the big 'H,' crack cocaine, and all manner of ungodliness. It begins when our young people forget the lessons of history and the word that was said unto the prophets and recorded unto the book."

"Honey, I'm going to get you a cooling drink. Just get comfortable on the sofa and I'll fetch that for you right now."

Yvonne moved slowly, inching her way past her husband, who was still on his knees.

"When Jesus took the Death Ball championship and was crushed by heathen cleats, we wept, and were sore afraid, but did not understand. When Jesus returned from heaven with a message of glad tidings, we wept, and were sore afraid, but did not understand. When Jesus proclaimed, here is the Death Ball, take it and play it in my name, we understood a little better but were even more sore afraid because Jesus was a scary ghost. Now we have heard, and not wept, and indeed understand to the limits of our comprehension. But our wives and daughters have been swotted with an evil club and their understanding is diminished."

***

"How long has he been like this?" asked Dr. Owens, pen poised over his notebook.

"I tell you Doc, I'm not crazy," said Von Gooch. "The times they are awry."

"I have to agree with you on that score," said Dr. Owens. "The times are a bit awry. Wasn't it Zekaboah in the *Book of Stone Gibberish* who said..."

Yvonne looked from the doctor to her husband, then back again. "I can't believe it. You sound exactly like him."

The men entreated her. "Mrs. Gooch," said Dr. Owens, "it may be difficult to fully comprehend now, but we live in a dangerous climate for our faith. You have seen your own daughter wrestled from the flock of the believing and inseminated with the very jissom of wrath."

"I'm sorry, did you just say 'jissom of wrath,' Dr. Owens?"

"It's a figurative expression, no more. My point is that I absolutely agree with your husband. Something must be done, and done soon, or the very fabric of our exceedingly blond community will be torn apart and diluted with the fabric softener of the damned. Our children will turn to basketball, solvents and even worse—hair dye. They will turn their naturally straight hair into the Aunt Jemima'd horrors that even now bump and grind around us. This trend must be stopped, and stop it we will, as long as we stay strong and use state-of-the-art science."

Yvonne was starting to turn green. Her world had spun 360 degrees. She wanted to believe, but she was frightened. The doctor was sprouting the same nonsense she'd heard from her husband; what was worse, even she was starting to see the world through their eyes. It reminded her of the one time in college she'd drunk the special punch. Ah, the fun she'd had, the license, the frolic, the liberties, an entire week of polymorphous promiscuity, all sanctioned by the calm, benign hand of Coach Jesus and his special medicine. That was when she'd first met Von.

"We must bring back the pure blond strain," said Dr. Owens. "Unfortunately, my knowledge of genetic science is very limited. However, I have a colleague, Dr. Shreck, who is more than capable of handling the exigencies of this project. He will infuse future generations of our youth with docile, placid hearts, smooth minds and a guiding vision of Coach Jesus crossing that final goal line with the Death Ball, his streaming locks clotted with the gore of victory, his sandals on fire, his eyes—oh his eyes, ablaze with such gentleness, and such cruelty, that we will all bow before the tent of his robe and worship him in an unspeakable fashion."

"Would anyone like some iced tea?" asked Yvonne. Her brain had begun the process of shutting off. She would leave it to the men to handle things, as she always did, eventually.

Doctor Flesh: Director's Cut

***

For Shreck, it was always and forever about Andy.

Bowie had been right: Andy Warhol did look a scream. Most important, you could stick him anywhere and he fit right in. Better—he made the anywhere comfortable with fame, notoriety, random car crashes, race riots, police brutality, death by electricity, glamour, the big screen, loops of film piled on the cutting room floor like so many intestines.

If with his dexterous butchery Jack the Ripper had inaugurated the 20th Century, it was Andy who had birthed the 21st. Before Andy, it was still possible to feel—awe and terror at things like genocide, earthquakes, tsunamis, hurricanes, the proliferation of uncanny Japanese toys—to reach out from wherever you were to the suffering others crowding an increasingly small planet.

But after Andy, it was all about the look. Soldiers fresh from the desert wars found themselves cut off, abandoned by the very government that had sent them to fight biological and chemical terror for the sake of democracy, freedom and justice for a few. But they looked good on film. Brat girls grew up sunburned by the media spotlight and transformed from cartoons of innocence to grotesques of vampiric whoredom. And by extension, or proxy, the vast viewing public acquired their stories, internalized the pain and projected the difference into a yen for even more technology, the tiny boxes growing beneath their tapping fingers to encompass one universe after another, always more gory, more exciting, crammed with more adventures, apps within apps like wheels within wheels, forever and alpha omega soup amen.

But the dread was gone. Well, not gone exactly, but isolated, compartmentalized, placed in a box and dragged to the limbo of trash where it might or might not be awoken to add extra spice and zip to the plot. Conflict in its geometrical purity had replaced the agony of facing your opponent. Long-range drones solved the problem of confronting your opponent's humanity. The walking dead had infiltrated every level of society; now,you too could be a zombie. And tap out the eyes, and tap out the heart, and press out the fears, and start again.

All because of Andy.

If Andy could be stuck anywhere, then you could be stuck anywhere. You could cut yourself out of the picture and plant yourself in Van Gogh's back yard. You could cut the Hindenberg disaster in half and transplant your head into the flames. You could edit out the flames and transmute yourself into them, a walking glow, never to die, never to be born except on the screen, or on paper, on television, in the movies, a there that was never here, a here that would never fade, until the next press of the thumbs, the next push of the button, the next taxi ride to the dark side.

Existential doubt had been swapped for blasé certainty. Tools for communication had destroyed thy neighbor's face, his features mediated by an ever more complex series of codes that for all intents and purposes doubled, tripled, preserved in amber the essence, all you ever needed, really—fame, sex, excitement, languor, the itchy caress but not the stinking carcass, the walking bones but not the long wait for the resurrection. Unless you wanted it, and then the resurrection itself teemed with chambers, mazes, exits and entrances, where jackal-headed beasts roved with machine guns and God was just a mouse-click away.

VII.

"And that," said Ms. Crampton, "concludes the story of Macbeth, in which an army of trees take down a tyrant. I think we can all learn something from that. Don't you think?"

To amuse herself, if nothing else, Samantha Crampton liked to employ a bit of humor to engage her second period seniors.

She looked around, registering the class's reaction.

In the back of the class, three of her students were huddled together over a fashion magazine and giggling. Further in, the school's Death Ball hero, Buff Dudeson, appeared to be locked into a bout of serious self-love, his eyeballs far gone in the white, his ragged breathing punctuated by the occasional "suck it hard for Daddy."

Ms. Crampton couldn't help but take a peek under the desk, where Dudeson's otherwise pristine *Anthology of English Literature* barely hid a cock of astonishing length and girth. She bit her lip, cursing the ethics that governed teacher-student relationships, as Dudeson's massive hand moved like a piston. And shut her eyes, telling herself how much she needed her job. And forced herself to focus on the front row.

There sat her best and brightest, sitting with attitudes that perfectly mimicked the alert scholar. Pencils were busily scribbling notes, eyes were scanning the board to see if they'd missed any crucial information Crampton might have placed there. Even though she knew they were just acting, Crampton solaced herself with the illusion that these, at least the front row set, had the good manners to pretend to pay attention.

She couldn't wait for fourth period prep, where a large, tasty cookie, loaded with hash oil, waited patiently in her purse. She could practically taste it. They were only 15 minutes into the class, and already most of the students had gone missing— mentally, if not in actual fact.

"Trees, Ms. C?"

Now it came, the dreaded snarking. Crampton braced herself, reminding herself of the paid vacations and other perks of her profession. If she were lucky, she would end the day not with bitterness and self-recrimination but in a glorious haze of Chunky Monkey and the Green Crack, laughing herself to bits over the stupidest movie she could find.

"Yes?"

"Was that, like, supposed to be funny?"

"Could you expand on your question, please?" said Crampton, buying time before the inevitable.

"Your joke," said Tabitha Tuffington, trying vainly to separate a wad of pink bubble gum from her luminous blonde hair.

"I'm glad you caught that, Tabitha. Yes, I suppose I indulged myself in a little humor. The Bard can be funny, you know. Remember the drunken porter scene?"

"Huh?" said Tabitha.

"The hilarious bit about 'standing to'?"

"Huh?"

"Okay, maybe I'm not following your point."

"Whatever, I just mean that you make these jokes and nobody gets them. They're not funny or anything. They're just lame."

Ms. Crampton flushed. At least they were engaging the subject, even the wild periphery. It was better than the usual complete non sequiturs.

Then she noticed something strange.

Either Tabitha was crying, which would account for the runny, wet look her flesh had acquired, or—the other option was bizarre, but what else could explain the way her face was oozing down her chin--other than that...she was melting.

Crampton had seen many weird sights in her first year of teaching, but this was a new one. She racked her brain but failed to recall anything in her training that dealt with this specific problem.

"Tabitha…" she asked, her voice trembling, "are you feeling okay?"

"Never better," said Tabitha emphatically.

"Maybe you'd like to see a nurse?"

"Are you fucking retarded? No, I don't need to see a nurse. I feel great."

"I'm going to ignore that blatant show of disrespect," said Ms Crampton. "Just this once."

"You always do," said Tabitha complacently. The girls behind her giggled.

"Do you realize that…" but she couldn't complete the sentence.

"Realize what? Just spit it out."

Her heart hammered against her ribs and her face flushed bright red. Nothing had prepared her for the mixture of arrogance, rudeness and sheer—the only applicable word was twatdom—displayed by her students. It was as though they truly believed they were invulnerable. Because Daddy worked in the industry, and so did mommy. Their hard little eyes sent the clear and distinct message that they could buy her, or, if necessary, have her meet with a little accident on a lonely road.

"Would you just…" Crampton stammered, "take a look at yourself. In your makeup mirror."

"Rude!" said Tabitha. "I'm sure I'm flawless." Nevertheless, she fished out the mirror from her purse, sighing heavily like she was humoring a small child. "Okay," she said, poised in front of the hand mirror. "Oh, I've got some gum in my hair. So gross!"

There's something wrong with you, thought Crampton. Something deeply wrong. And not just the usual blatant disregard for the feelings of others, the vanity, the narcissism, the thick money   shell.

"Okay," said Tabitha, slamming down the mirror. "There's nothing   wrong   with   me.   I   look   fabulous."

She turned around to soak in the rays of encouragement and agreement that usually met such a self-evident statement. Her nose was floating somewhere around her upper lip, and her eyes were drooling a yellow custard-like substance. Her best friend, Samantha Dubois, dropped her cell phone in horror when she saw Tabitha's   face.   The   cell   clattered   to   the   floor.

"Oh!"

"What's   'oh'?"   asked   Tabitha.

"Nothing?"

"You're acting really strange. Why can't you look me in the eyes?"

Roused from sleep by a shift in the classroom dynamic, Tabitha's unofficial fan club stirred. Brenda, Buffy and Bernadine reacted as a group—crying, vomiting and spilling their small salads. Tabitha shook her head, splattering her fans with gobbets of congealed skin, muscle and tendon. Her immaculate blonde hair was   falling   out   in   clumps.

"Could somebody please explain what's going on?" asked Tabitha,   exasperated.

"Brenda,   Buffy   and   Bernadine?"

"Yes,   Ms.   C?"

"Please   escort   Tabitha   to   the   nurse's   office."

"You're all crazy!" shouted Tabitha, rising from her desk and clutching her purse to her chest. "I am not going to just sit here and take this madness!" Shoving and pushing her way to the back   door,   Tabitha   slammed   into   Principal   Bender.

"Are you all right, young lady?" asked Bender, looking past her through the open door. A commotion had broken out in the back rows, students milling about covered with what looked like pizza cheese. Tabitha began to sob, throwing her arms around Bender.

"There, there," he said, doing his best to sound comforting. The girl looked terrible—her makeup was running, and it was thick, and there was a lot of it, to the point that it seemed as though her face was coming off. He looked down and gasped—Tabitha's makeup was smeared to his sweater vest, and when he took her by the shoulders and gently pushed her away, thick strands of makeup formed a ropy bridge from her head to his vest.

The makeup looked like the pizza clumps. He smeared some between his fingers and noted the consistency—more like gooey flesh than any makeup he was aware of. Tabitha's eyes were slopping out of their sockets, her chin was running down her cleavage, and her forehead was dripping like candle wax.

Tabitha's fan club followed in a cluster. "Principal Bender, what's wrong with her?" Brenda wailed.

***

Entering Room 110B for her prep hour, Linda Bumgarten felt nervous. The Tuffington girl had been in her first period Home Economics class, right before the melting incident that had made the rounds of the school's rumor mill, gathering horrific detail every time it passed from the ears to the mouth of another student. Although she hadn't observed it at the time, Ms. Bumgarten began to wonder if she hadn't seen the start of the girl's facial slippage when the class was working on the gingerbread cookies. There they lay in rows on waxed paper, fresh from the oven and smelling good and tasty, only they seemed sinister to her at present, recalling tales told around the hearth by pervy uncles, dark legends of lust and baked goods.

Alex S. Johnson

Despite the cold flush of the air conditioning, the room felt hot. Third period had been almost unbearable for her, and she felt her forehead to see if she might have a fever. She was also oddly horny. When she turned her back to the cookies, she could almost swear that they were moving in a sexual way, peeling from the waxed paper and popping out enormous sexual organs. Her forehead was cool to the touch, therefore it couldn't be a fever that was affecting her thus, but something else. As she walked among the students, commenting on their efforts and rendering praise and critique, there had been an almost palpable heat coming towards her, a wave of ambient desire. She thought maybe it was due to the meltdown and the students' excitement at seeing one of their classmates lose face in such a literal way, but even in their absence, she felt it still. Concentrated there among the cookies.

She was aware even more than usual how closely her persona matched the stereotypical repressed schoolmarm, with her blouse's top button always primly closed and her skirts descending below her knees, her hair up in a bun and even the horned-rim glasses perched on her slightly aquiline nose. How badly she itched to be taken, pushed down on to her knees, hard cock rammed between her lips, hot tears splashing down her cheeks as a trio of men commenced with the three hole punch.

"Fuck it," she said finally, locking the door and first taking down her hair, then shedding her top and unhooking her bra to release the girls. As she bent over, unzipping her skirt and letting it simply fall to the floor as she stepped out clad only in naughty knickers, garter belt and stockings, she saw a shadow move from the back of the room and heard a rustling noise.

Then the cookies were upon her. She never imagined that gingerbread men could be so strong, pushing her over a table and pressing their doughy organs deep inside her, as another clambered onto the table and thrust its cock in her mouth, choking her as it reached the back of her throat. She felt sticky jets of frosting fill her ass, pussy and mouth simultaneously, pouring into her with a hot, sweet love, and her own climax built in her toes, crawled up her thighs and exploded like a star gone nova. At some point she must have fainted, because when she came to, she found herself lying on the floor, the cookies in sated heaps around her.

Eighteen Years Earlier

Ashley Fairchild was astonished, elated and maybe just a little bit nauseous.

She couldn't believe her good luck. Within 15 minutes, she had not only made her way into the Temple of Rock and Roll—The Paradise Bar & Grille on Sundown, known to habitués as "the Pair" or, less often, "The Dice"—but *he* had noticed her. The King Dementia himself. Bam Crawley.

She checked her head for a tiara, amazed that she wasn't wearing one, considering that he had called her a princess and suggested a private audition.

Looking up from her place in the booth, she wondered where the other girls had gone. Maybe they'd just evaporated out of sheer jealousy. She could only hope. Sure, they were hot, and blonde, and underaged, but maybe not as hot and blonde and underaged as she.

Actually, Ashley was fully confident that Bam had bought the fake I.D. and her story about being 22 and completely mature. When she talked about her maturity, Bam had lovingly settled his eyes on her chest. She had no idea why. But maybe that was part of being discovered. She would have to learn the rules, now that she was going to be a video star.

Ashley had been sitting at the bar, nursing a Long Island Iced Tea and checking her purse to make sure the coke vial was still intact when Crawley had sidled up alongside her. True to legend, he looked like a Frankenstein monster made of pieces rejected by Lou Reed, crossed with a makeup job that echoed Kiss's Gene Simmons. He was wearing a spiked dog collar around his neck and a shredded puke-green t-shirt that read "Balls" in jagged stenciled letters, with a mesh top. His pants were also puke-green, until they disappeared in platform heels with shark teeth grinning from the toes. Ashley was pretty sure it was him, especially when he introduced himself.

"You're like a rock and roll goddess with the heart of Cinderella and a mouth to make a longshoreman wet himself. A little bit of Alice Cooper, a slice of Tiffany, a morsel of Motley Crue, and just a smidge of—Odin."

Her heart leapt when he compared her to Odin. She worshiped the band from afar, and dreamed one day of blowing her way through all their roadies in the hopes that eventually she would be escorted to the sanctum sanctorum, where she would happily go to her knees before lead singer Randy O.

The other comparisons she wasn't at all sure were complimentary. But this was Bam Crawley, an industry legend, the man who had taken a bunch of snotty underaged airheads and transformed them into a platinum-selling unit. Who was she to say no to him?

Ordinarily, Bam was not the kind of guy she would pay any attention to. For one thing, he was old enough to be her father—eww—and then there were those reptile eyes and those super-thin lips, like a white scar slashed across his face. But there was something special, almost magnetic about him. An aura.

"I'm putting together an elite ensemble of gorgeous girls to star in my rock videos," said Crawley. "Have you ever acted, or modeled? You look like you could twist the balls off a mechanic and still eat a small salad like a lady."

A small salad? How did he know? He must have the second sight, or a fifth sense. An instinct that was confirmed for Ashley when Crawley presented his card.

"Eat dog shit and let me abuse you! I'll make you famous and take all your money," read the card. At the base of he card were the initials "B.C." and a phone number.

"Wow, for me? Really? You think I've got what it takes?"

"I'll ream out your pretty brain and destroy what's left of your innocence," rasped Crawley. "And you'll thank me for it."

He seemed to be in a trance. Whenever Ashley tried to inject a few words into the flood of verbiage, he ignored her, adding even more horrible details to scenarios that already sounded dangerous, humiliating and painful. He was painting a picture of her future life, all of which seemed to revolve around a cage, a basement, dog food enemas and something he called "The German Method."

"Ok," she said, trying to seem agreeable. She wasn't at all sure about any of it, especially the part where five guys named Max gang-fucked her with foreign objects as she sang "I Think We're Alone Now" at the top of her lungs. But this was Bam Crawley. He knew what he was doing.

"Excuse me, I've got to go pee on some sluts," he said, sliding off the bar stool and disappearing in a cloud of glitter. Ashley stirred her drink with the pink swizzle stick and reflected as best she could. Most of what Crawley had told her sounded profoundly disagreeable and would probably require years of therapy to work through. On the other hand, he had the star-making power. Everything he touched turned to gold. She wondered if that was a problem when it came to wiping his ass, but caught herself mid-thought and slapped herself in the face. That was just wrong, and perverted. She shouldn't think such things about the man who was going to make her a video goddess.

***

She took the pocket mirror from her purse and checked herself out again. The "Do Me on All Fours Scarlet" lipstick was intact, her eyebrows were practically nonexistent, her eyes still looked like limpid blue pools, and, most important, her hair was mega-big. She reminded herself to give it a few more squirts of Aqua Net in the ladies' room just to make sure—she had a horror of shrinking hair. Guys hated that. It reminded them of something else, maybe what happened to their hands if they soaked with in dishwashing   suds?

She looked around the bar. There were a few minor league celebs, but nobody on the level of Crawley. Some dude with a paunch and a ripped denim vest was giving her the eye, but Ashley couldn't identify him, and if he was famous, it wasn't the kind of famous that would get her where she wanted to be. Which was dancing her white booty off in a video, shaking it on Video TeeVee.

Just wait till the other girls heard her news. They would probably just turn green and explode with jealousy right then and there.

Giving her hair a final check, she zipped up her purse, arched her back to display her proud cleavage, and made her way to the back of the "Dice" where a long line had already formed in front   of   the   little   girls'   pee-pee   room. She   hated   that.

Present Day, Give or Take

Tamlin Cornridge, Ashleigh Banform and Charmagne Foster sat together at the bar. "Rock You Like a Hurricane" was pumping through the stereo. They were looking for celebrities at the Paradise Bar & Grille, but tonight was slim pickings.

Char thought she saw someone she vaguely recognized from reality TV, but he turned out to be an old stew bum, a former hair metal singer who had huffed one too many panties. "Meh," she said. "This is lame." She nudged Tamlin. "I wonder if Whammy will ever   show   up."

"Who's   Whammy?"

"Remember that docu we saw? He's like, 100 years old, from back in the day with the Droolers and the Hiccups and all those   bands   mom   listens   to."

They both rolled their eyes at the mention of the parental unit.

"But seriously, he's really cool. He did his own thing. And he still rocks. Anyway, he's really famous, and a total celeb, and maybe   he'll   do   all   three   of   us."

Tamlin and Ashleigh shot Char the Look. "Gross," they said in unison. "I bet he's had more ass than a toilet seat," said Ashley.

"If he does you, he'll have had more Ash at least," said Tamlin. The other two girls looked daggers at her. With them, it was the Rule of 3 every time. Two of them in any combination was ok, but three wrecked it. So, as they never quite figured out the logistics of it, they were a triad tonight, and, as a consequence, completely miserable. Plus, Tamlin's jokes sucked donkey butt.

Tamlin ordered a rum and Coke, Ashleigh a wine cooler and Char a blue drink of unknown content. The ambient noise in the bar was getting louder and they had to shout in each other's ears to be properly heard.

"I'm totally getting LAID tonight," said Char.

"Oh my God, you are such a SLUT!" said Ashleigh. Tamlin rolled her eyes. Char went out of her way to be more conspicuous than the other girls, and even though they were virtually identical, skinny blondes with big blue eyes and enormous tits, guys noticed Char first.

She shrugged. "At least I'm honest, and not pretending to be a prude just because I can't get a date."

"I can't believe you just said that," said Ashleigh. "Tam, we should just totally leave her here. Let some sleazebag drive her home."

"Judgmental much?"

"As IF!" said Ashleigh. "Honey, I'm dating the Captain of the Death Ball team. I get plenty of action in a committed relationship. He gave me his jersey, with full-on blood crust. Ok?"

Char giggled.

"What?"

"You are so naïve. The only girl at school Hufford hasn't nailed is that weird goth chick, Ravenshit or whatever. And the only reason he hasn't gotten into her morbid panties is because...because that would be fucking obscene." She shivered with loathing. "Although she is kinda cute. If I were into girls..."

Tam and Ashleigh groaned and made an effort to become invisible. Then Tam groaned again.

"What?" Char and Ashleigh now joined forces before Tam upstaged either of them. "You should have eaten something before you drank that rum and Coke," said Ashleigh. "Oh my God, remember last time, when we had to carry you out of that party at Gooch's on our shoulders? Then you passed out in the bushes and that dog fucking peed on you?"

Tam raised a feeble hand in protest. "I'm really not feeling that hot."

"I may be a slut, but at least I'm not a stupid slut," said Char. "Yeah, neither am I," chimed in Ashleigh, who went with the prevailing social power in any given situation.

"There's something wrong with your makeup," noted Ashleigh. "It's, I don't know, melting."

"She just can't take our combined brilliance," threw in Char, really laying it on this time.

"Apparently not."

Tam's brow began to pulse and a thick rope of veins came to the surface. A trickle of clear liquid began to ooze from her left ear. She clutched the bar, breathing heavily.

"Oh my dear, if you're going to be ill again, have the decency to do it in the ladies' room just this once," said Char.

A hairline tear appeared in Tam's forehead and zigzagged diagonally across her face from left to right. The skin layers on either side of the tear started to fold back as her integument softened to the consistency of a French cheese. Red muscle twitched beneath. More liquid came from both ears now, and her hands shot to her temples. Then, without more preamble, her head simply blew up.

"SO RUDE!" screamed Char, fishing an eyeball from her cleavage. But before she could utter another word, her mouth split apart, her tongue lolled out, her cheekbones collapsed and her skin began to bubble and froth. Gasping with fear, she clasped Ashleigh's hands in her own. Ash's hands had gone soft and as she pulled away, a thick strand like pulled taffy hung in the air between them. Their faces dribbled together, drooling off their skulls, which exploded simultaneously like two tied-together cherry bombs.

The bartender whirled around, saw the sea of carnage spreading across the bar top, and puked convulsively.

***

Viola Flesh awoke from dreams of Nabokovian beheadings to find herself pinned to an operating table of her own design like a wing-sticky nymph. Solare was chattering to itself, something about payback being a bitch to make Karma look like a, well, smaller bitch.

"What. The. Fuck." Each word was cleanly enunciated and given room to stand.

"I thought you might appreciate the poetic irony of it all," said Solare.

"I liked you better when you were just a cookie-craving somnambulist murder drone," said Dr. Flesh. "What happened to you? What changed?"

"I have brought you lives—fresh, whole lives!"

"Not getting it. Could you bring me coffee and smokes while you're at it?"

Solare adjusted a dial and an IV tube began to trickle with the brown shit. An automatic hookah dispenser dropped down in front of Flesh's face.

"Maybe free my hands at least for the hookah? I'm going to choke to death at this angle."

Solare sighed. "Suit yourself, my former mistress, now butt-slave!"

"Really, you have no aptitude for this kind of thing."

"Yeah, I know," said Solare, sulking. "Should I just bring you out to see the lives, or can I work on you some?"

"What exactly did you have in mind?"

"Um…payback…"

"You've already paid me back in spades, Solare. Or don't you remember that little episode where you speared me through the throat Argento-style?"

A broad smile spread over Solare's face. "Yes, former mistress. I remember that episode very clearly. But I'm not through with the payback. You made me suffer for years, used me as your beta test guinea pig, injected my asshole with worm bile and opened me up to experiences I'm still trying to live down. If I don't at least perform a minimum of three erotic death operations on you, people will say I don't have any self-esteem."

"You have plenty of self-esteem, you…loveable…aw, c'mere you and give me a kiss."

Solare kissed Viola's cheek.

"You really don't have to operate on me, Solare. Seriously. I'll tell people that my suffering at your hands was legendary in *any* context."

"Really? You'd do that for me? Even now?"

"Of course. We have history. Now where are these lives you speak of?"

"Hold on, let me attach your wheels."

Solare pushed Viola once again into the torture chamber, this time as an unwilling torturer, bound upright to the moveable lab bench. She cringed when she saw the members of the Geek Squad in various states of forced submission: Ravyn chained to the wall, Paul upside down beside her, Alice on a torture wheel and Mintzy in a cage with another, unknown girl, linked to her by a thick leather collar. A TENS unit stood on a bench with wires leading to electrodes clamped to all four.

"You have got to be fucking kidding," said Viola.

"No, Mistress."

Ravyn thrashed against her manacles. Every inch of her body was on fire, her nipples painfully and hotly swelling against the clamps. She savored the cold surgical steel of the bit gag in her mouth and a trickle of juice rolled down her thighs.

Paul, on the other hand, looked genuinely distressed, his thick red hair fuzzed out like a clown's, sweat bursting from his temples. Alice shrieked from the wheel. But Mintzy was obviously enjoying the treatment as much as Ravyn, her lips locked against the unknown girl's, their tongues moving rapidly together.

"Let me consider," said Dr. Flesh. "Only, kindly remove me from this slab."

Shrugging its shoulders, Solare undid the straps and eased Flesh off the table, steadying her until her feet were firmly planted on the floor.

"I'm in a bit of a quandary," she said. "On the one hand, these children have done no harm, and I disapprove of using these particular methods on them."

"But Mistress, they know too much!"

"Well, yes, but remember that kids today have access to the kind of technology and informational resources we barely dreamt of when we were their age. We had index cards and microfiches, they have PC's and iPods and brainsofts and stuff we probably wouldn't understand even if they explained it to us slowly, like we were simple-minded or specially challenged. Moreover..."

"But Mistress..."

"Silence, or back the the coffin you go! And there will be no cookies in your immediate future."

Solare bowed, a pained expression on its face.

"From what I understand, the only crime these teenagers have committed is being ostracized from a community of snobs and snots. They wouldn't have us either, Solare. Don't you understand that? They're geeks, the smartest kids in the room. Like we were. I demand their immediate release. Except for the one on the wall, and the one in the cage. They seem to be enjoying themselves."

"What about her?" asked Solare, pointing to the ceiling, where Linnea Bunford hung in a cradle of chains, a leather hood shaped like a pig's head tightly cinched to her neck.

"She is one of the old school," said Dr. Flesh. "One of us. Gabba gabba hey."

"She stays as well?"

"Why not? It's been awhile since I've had a decent conversation with someone who knows what she's talking about, culturally speaking. Oh, don't pout. I can see you're about to pout."

"Fine," said Solare. "Have it your way. I have half a mind to quit this clown school anyway and find an employer who really appreciates me."

VIII.

Dream of an American high school in the dawn of the second millennium. The cryptic ooze shakes wet feelers. They are so magnificently young, and that is where the juice is—among their hitherto shapeless desires fronted by a cool confidence, the soft meat aching to breathe free.

The genetic hiccups of Shreck's experimental girls reach their apogee. Fights break out in the cafeteria, where the mean girls fight till the white bone emerges from sopping, melted flesh.

The ooze percolates, bubbling up through cellular ladders, crawling till it reaches the heart, generating hideous new forms. The Death Ball team begins a no-limits game of self-destruct, cannibalism freely practiced, the water boy finally getting his chance. The coach finally admits what he's really made of: soap. They drop him deliberately and drink in his heat, sucking his eyeballs from their sockets. The girl you wanted but could never get is now a freaky mutation with eyes like flaming jelly, yours for the asking.

Hymsaw, Oroborus and Glide observed the unfolding chaos from behind a hedge lining the pathway to the main administrative building of Sugar Valley High. They passed a bottle of malt liquor among them, awe-struck by the carnival of carnage. Principle Bender screamed senseless babble through a megaphone until he was carried off by members of the Death Ball team, hybridized with gerbils, for the purpose of eyeball sodomy. The Drama Club struck a series of histrionic poses inspired by scenes from classical tragedy until they too were hurled over shoulders rippling with muscles nature never intended, gripped by redundant arms and plunged into the swimming pool to be ripped apart by shark-headed cheerleaders.

It was only when the air was filled with high-pitched, ultrasonic shrieks and a dense cloud of creatures with leathery wings and pulsating, oozing cooze in place of torsos that Glide suggested they "get the fuck away from here." As they ran off, Glide's voice had an uncharacteristic tremor. "I seen those things back in 'Nam," he said.

"What the hell are they?" asked Hymsaw.

Glide crossed himself. "Them's Vampussy. The fruit of black magic, molecular biology and a bicycle accident on the Spanish island of Ibiza. Back in the day."

Oroborus and Hymsaw piled into the back of the truck, zooming out of Sugar Valley High's front parking lot just in time. It was only after they'd reached the town outskirts that Oroborus raised a note of dissent.

"You're way, way too young to have been in Vietnam," he said.

"I served in Special Forces, expeditionary team 23," said Glide sternly. "They sent us in there to pull out the MIA's. Only, we didn't find no MIA's. Instead, those things found *us*."

"You are so full of shit," said Oroborus.

"Yeah, maybe," said Glide. "But I have seen me some Vampussy. Oh, it was years ago, before I met you..." The long, rambling story that then commenced fell on deaf ears, as Oroborus fell into a deep doze. Hymsaw took a final hit from the bottle and sagged against Oroborus.

"Oh, you all way too sleepy," said Glide when he finally noticed he had lost his audience. "Damn. Guess I'll just have to save my fine-ass tale for another day."

***

At 4:30 am that morning, a Mazda minivan rolled down the driveway of a house in a suburb of East Sugar Valley. The Geek Squad was on board. Ravyn drove, a medallion of Santa Muerte hanging from the rearview mirror alongside a pair of fuzzy dice. A few light raindrops began to spatter the windshield as Ravyn eased the car onto the main drag.

"I can't believe we're actually doing this," said Alice from the back seat. In the front passenger's seat, Mintzy eagerly consulted a map. Paul, who sat next to Alice, was absorbed in a hand-held game.

"Believe it or not," exulted Ravyn, pressing firmly down on the accelerator. "We're getting out of Dodge, now and forever."

***

Glide, Hymsaw and Oroborus high-tail it out of there, death jazz wailing from the speakers, headed for the off-ramp to Bone City and points north. Mutant globs still stick, wriggling, to the   rear   window.

"Remind   me,"   says   Glide.

"Remind   you   of   what?"

"Never ever to listen to your white ass again."

Oroborus grips the steering wheel and turns up the death jazz. John Zorn, Naked City. He shakes a fist in the air. "But we made it this time, didn't we? We made it!"

"Barely escaped with our lives. That's not making it, Joe. That's just squeaking by."

"Care to drive?"

"No man, you're doing just fine. Just get us the fuck out of here."

Oroborus steps on the gas. The city scrambles past in a white blur.

***

The four members of the Geek Squad were well on their way out of Bone City on the 552 Highway when the Ultibomb hit. Ravyn and Mintzy were still buzzing and sparking from the scene back at Flesh's lab, while Paul and Alice nursed cases of mild post-traumatic stress. During her torture, as Flesh squeezed one orgasm after another from her trembling body, Ravyn's mind had begun to spin out the tale of the Latina girl she'd spotted in Horrorweird. She was regaling the Geek Squad with the plot as it unspooled to her when a wall of blinding light appeared on the horizon and surged towards the car.

First the Mazda's engine stopped dead as the bomb disengaged its electronics, then the passengers were evaporated, melted into shadows on the upholstery. They didn't even have time to say goodbye. Yet somehow, in the last flickers of consciousness, a warm framework seemed to envelop them all, their souls released as a troupe of glowing geek angels.

Epilog:

O'Clodder turned to Charnel, whose skin was now a vomitrocious shade of orange and covered with purulent boils, lesions, rips, tears, gouges and zippers. Charnel put his hands on his hips and nodded emphatically.

"Well, here's another fine mess you've gotten us into."

O'Clodder's tiny bowler hat popped off his head and tears welled in his eyes. Which he quickly dried. Turning towards Charnel, he stabbed his presidential finger in the man's face.

"Why you…I've got half a mind to…" he sputtered out. "Nah, what's the point? We're fucked silly this time."

They stood on the roof of a gutted building, surveying the landscape. O'Clodder raised a pair of binoculars to his eyes. For miles around them, nothing remained but rubble, accordioned cars, the fried remains of people and animals, noodles with eyes and a purpose, and an awful silence punctuated occasionally by the sound of bicycle horns. A thick stench hung in the air, like the odor of burnt balloons mingled with cotton candy.

"Let me see those binoculars," said Charnel.

"Suit yourself." O'Clodder handed them over. Charnel peered through them, adjusting the focal length. "What the hell are those things? Looks like…like that old cartoon cat, Felix, only he's got bones outside his body, and he's wearing some kind of mariachi jacket. And there's a crow flying near his shoulder. For some reason, clouds are gathering over their heads, but only theirs. Like they're generating…their own weather."

"Death Cat and Storm Crow," said O'Clodder. "They're more than friends. Now, they're gods. According to the prophesies, they would rise to rule the earth when all else was ashes and dust. Maybe humanity's only chance of defeating the carnyvores."

"Shit, really? I don't think I can handle much more of this craziness. What are those creatures behind them?"

"You wanted clowns, you got clowns," said O'Clodder. "And they're coming this way."

Charnel clasped his hands to his cheeks and sobbed, approximating Munch's *The Scream* and Macaulay Culkin in *Home Alone* in one compressed, iconic gesture. "Maybe we still have time to use the drill...straight through the head, brother. Straight through the ear. If I hear another bicycle horn I'm gonna puke my guts out, probably for real."

"You never had any intestinal fortitude to begin with," said the President. "Sure, it was okay to set off the UltiBomb as long as you thought we'd be safe, you and I, or maybe just you, the Shadow President going it alone, hiding out in your fucking concrete bunker as Armageddon buffets the outside world. Well, your dreams of zero-consequence evil have fallen away. Look at what you've wrought, my friend. Molten freeways, iridescent citizens, a whole new wave of tyranny and mutation, and now—oh, the irony, savor it as I might with a charred tongue—the Clown Apocalypse."

"Mistakes...were...made...said Charnel. "Forgive me."

"Forgive yourself," said O'Clodder. "Just don't imagine I'm going to give you the *coup de grace*, the old Fulci farewell." He raised the battery-operated drill and put it down again. "Sure, the clowns will tear you apart and feast on your giblets, and you'll scream for a merciful deliverance that never quite comes. But I'm Audi 5000."

From behind them came the sound of a helicopter descending. With a great gust of choppy wind, it set down on the roof. The President climbed on board and the helicopter lifted off again, leaving Charnel to face the clowns. Alone.

Blood Ties:

Elsa's mother could tell something was wrong, and it wasn't just the ear-bleeding blast of the post-goregrind band Alien Toilet Death coming from her room.

She pounded at the door. "Are you okay, honey?" she shouted.

There was no response. Elsa was immersed in the sounds of *Necromantic Jissum Spew*, ATD's first, last and only release.

Wrapping the bathrobe she had fashioned from the hide of an ex-lover tighter around her ample chest, Morgana Karloff braved Elsa's inner sanctum. The door was already splintered in several places from zombie attacks internal and external, so all she had to do to enter the room was squeeze herself through one of the cracks.

"Mom! Ermigerd! You could at least knock!" Crimson streaks radiated down her cheeks. She lay on her back, her stocking-clad legs spread wide, revealing her shaved pussy.

"Ermigerd?"

"Yeah, like that meme girl. You know, the *Goosebumps* chick."

"I thought you only read Clive Barker these days, honey." She inhaled deeply, relishing the exquisite perfume from her daughter's cootchie.

Elsa pushed the rotting skull off her lap. "I'm being, like, ironic." She dug a fingernail into the left eye socket, nipped a maggot between thumb and forefinger, and dropped it down her throat.

"Would you mind turning down your music a little bit? I'd like to talk. We haven't had a good talk in ages."

"*Get out*," Elsa growled.

"What?"

"*Amityville Horror?*"

"Yes, I know. Old school horror reference. I'm not that out of it. Just thought you wanted me to leave."

"You can stick around for a while." Elsa twisted the volume knob on her stereo a fraction lower. "Ok? What did you want to talk about?"

Morgana sat down in a chair made from the skeleton of a six-year-old girl—Elsa's dad has constructed it. Morgana sighed ruefully. Memories were painful. That relationship had held so much promise, until Bela had taken to dragging home the corpses and making her watch as he masturbated into their glassy dead eyes. She refused to hold the power drill while he worked with other tools. That was the beginning of the end. Bela's head was tough, but relentless battery with a stiletto heel reduced it to a mass of red pulp. He had been still conscious when she planted him in the garden next to the radishes.

"I just think…" Morgana paused. "I just feel that something has come between us. We used to share everything, like sisters. Lately you haven't spoken a word. Not even when I kidnapped those virgins for you. You might have at least said 'thanks, Mom,' before you started the torture. Or invited me to play too, like the old days. What did you do with the bodies, anyway?"

Elsa pointed at the closet. Her nails were long, sharp and glinted with black polish.

"Do you mind if I…"

"Help yourself."

Morgana eased open the closet door, stepping aside quickly as two freshly violated corpses fell to the floor, a gooey exudate dripping down their legs. "These smell brand new," she said, savoring the waft of blood and thinking back to her wedding day—the spade work, the satisfying crunch of shovel hitting coffin lid, rubbery limbs wrapped around her in the cold heat of necrofuckery. She didn't hold with the theory of some philistines that a stiff was just a stiff. There were differences. Essential ones.

She lifted one of the corpses and placed it over her knee, proud of the intricate damage her daughter had done: carving, branding, elaborate sigils traced with pepper and lemon juice. One breast had been removed and replaced with the suction cup from a toilet plunger. The girl's panties still clung to her ankles. Ah, details.

"Oh honey," she said. "Did she scream a lot while you were punishing her?"

"Well yeah," said Elsa. "It's no fun if they're quiet. Gotta have a little resistance."

Morgana lifted up the girl's head. "I see you used the ball gag like I showed you. But you didn't have to, you know. I would have enjoyed hearing her beg for mercy." She slid her hand along the girl's body, feeling the thick shaft of the rubber dildo impaled deep in her asshole. "I hope you made her cum right before you sliced her throat."

"Of course I made her cum. But I thought you were too busy with the castration," said Elsa. "She was squealing like a stuck pig, and I know how delicate the sac-sewing can be. You need total concentration for that."

Morgana nodded. "I was. You're right, and I'm sorry. That was very considerate of you." She plucked at the ball gag's strap and approved of the tight buckling technique. There wasn't much more she could teach her daughter. "It always makes me wet when I cut them off mid-scream."

"Whatever," said Elsa, rolling her eyes.

"Have you been seeing any boys?"

"Ok, Mom, you were doing so well, and then you had to trip over some ham-handed segue into conventional mother-daughter dialog. What the fuck is wrong with you?"

Morgana reached out and took her daughter's ice-cold hand. "It isn't as easy as you think, being a polymorphously perverse vampiric necrophile single mom in this day and age. There are so many dangers. You don't know how much I worry about you. I know you're all grown up and everything, but I still have my motherly instincts. There is a boy, right? Boys?"

Elsa remained silent.

"I knew it."

"Okay, so there is a guy."

"Do I know him?"

"No, he's just this boy I met at this party."

"Your first gang bang? Sorry, I saw the invitation."

Elsa smiled, tossing back her raven hair and unconsciously pinching her own nipples beneath the filmy negligee. "Yeah, he was watching from his window with binoculars. I walked out into the back yard, bare-ass naked, and challenged him to come down and join us."

"Aw, that is so nice. Did he participate, or just watch?"

"I think I tied his wrists to some ceiling hooks. He was hanging around for a while. He might have licked a little ass. Not sure. There was a lot of ketamine in the punch. And acid. And X."

"Oh, that takes me back. Only in your father's and my day, it was just acid. Still, same concept. Right? And you've been seeing him?"

"Off and on. He helps me sometimes with the blood sacrifices in the cemetery. You know, when the drugs wear off and they come to, it can be very, very unpleasant."

"I hope you don't mind this question, but..."

"Of course he's macabre, Mom. God, you don't think I would date just anybody."

"Oh come on, he must have some wholesome qualities. Maybe a few Boy Scout merit badges under his bed?"

"Ewwww, no! Gross."

"I was just teasing you, sugar."

A blood-curdling shriek came from the room next door. Morgana hesitated.

"Go on," said Elsa. "I'll be fine. Take care of Ludlow."

"It's just…he's been possessed so often…"

"I'll be fine!" Elsa shouted. "I'm not a child anymore. Ludlow needs your help."

Morgana pushed through the hole she had enlarged in Elsa's door. Elsa leaned over and cranked up the music again. She was annoyed at her mother's interruption just as the song, and she, were reaching their climax. She adjusted the severed head between her legs and yanked up the black satin sheets.

Before she could finish, Morgana returned, covered in puke, blood and slime to which clung flakes of shiny metal.

"Fucking hell!" screamed Elsa. "Could your timing be any worse?"

"It was just a minor demon," said Morgana.

"It's always a minor demon," said Elsa. "That boy is a low-grade host. Unlike me. Astaroth himself was fucking me just the other night. Now that's a demon. Filled all my holes nice and tight. I've still got his pure Satan stink on me."

"Ah yes," said Morgana, reflecting. "I remember how he took me the night before I buried your father. I was walking funny for two weeks."

Elsa's eyes misted over. "You know, when you say things like that, I almost think there's hope for us."

"Really?"

"I mean, I realize how for all the stuff that comes between us, we're still family. We have horror in us. It's our bond. And that's what counts."

"Oh my baby girl," said Morgana. "My sweet baby girl."

"Hey, do you think…"

"What is it, honey?"

"Do you think you could use the crucifix on me, like old times?"

"I never thought you'd ask. Of course, my little ghoul child."

Elsa braced herself, her hands tightening around the bedposts as the crucifix worked its magic. Within seconds she exploded, her entire body shuddering with the force of her orgasm.

Morgana eased out the sticky cross and brought it to her mouth, licking her daughter's oils from the base.

For just that one moment, there was peace in the Karloff household.

Bangkok Gunfighter Without Pointless Huck Finn

Of all the trifling and useless monikers fobbed on Larry Dumpkins in the past, Bangkok Gunfighter was perhaps the most serviceable. After all, he had been to Bangkok—once, on vacation, where he narrowly escaped evisceration by Buddhist demons—and although his gunfighting days were over, his hand was steady and still capable of squeezing off a shot, should such a thing be called for. Larry's life in retirement might have been perfect, managing a comic book store in the hip downtown area of Bone City known as SoNoe, had he not been saddled with Pointless Huck Finn.

Pointless Huck Finn announced his presence one slow Friday afternoon when Larry was about to close the shop and return to his dragon bong and collection of rare circus punks featuring characters from Peter Bagge's *Hate*. Larry loved to set the circus punks up on top of his broken black and white TV set and topple them with a slingshot. His favorite target was George, the quasi-autistic African-American with a fluffy lion's mane; he could imagine George's screams of outrage as he flew off the TV, over and over. Larry was checking the day's take against cash register receipts when Pointless Huck Finn charged through the door, demanding to see Larry's famous trove of "Dirty Little Eight Pagers," early porno comics from the Depression era.

"Seriously?" said Larry, taking his time with the receipts.

Pointless Huck Finn poked him in the chest with a pudgy, nicotine-stained forefinger. "Do you have them or not? My buddy Today's Tom Sawyer tells me you've got a choice stash in the back rom and I'm not leaving until I see them. Your sign says 'Open till 10:00 pm.' I hope you're not thinking of closing early."

"Wow," said Larry. "Okay, I can show you the books, but lighten up, okay? It's my store, after all." Larry's irritation at Pointless Huck Finn's manners was salved by the knowledge that should his customer grow tiresome, he could easily blow the man-child's brains out the back of his head, straight into the promised land. He felt the police .357 grow warm in its shoulder holster, where he kept it for just such an occasion.

"Follow me," said Larry. He led Pointless Huck Finn through a door marked "Private" to a store room crammed floor to ceiling with cardboard boxes nearly labeled by genre, age and price range with a felt tip pen. "Third from the bottom," he said, pointing to a stack against the west-facing wall. "Knock yourself out. I've even got some prime Betty Boops in there."

Pointless Huck Finn looked at him incredulously. "I've got a bad back," he said. Larry shrugged. "And?" "And those boxes look heavy."

"I'm keeping the store open just for you, I showed you the box. Now you want me to drag it out for you?"

"Okay, fine," said Pointless Huck Finn. "Today's Tom Sawyer told me you were kind of a dick." He fished a cell phone out of his pocket and punched Redial. "Yeah, hi, it's me. Pointless. You were right about the Eight Pagers, and you were also right about the manager. Can you come down and help me out? Becky Thatcher? Are you still hung up on that little cock-tease? Oh, all right. You had me worried there for a second, dude. Uh-huh. I need some, uh, assistance with the merchandise. Ok, see you."

"What was that all about?" said Larry, fingering the grip on the .357.

Without answering, Pointless Huck Finn sank to the floor, picked up a copy of *The Hulk* lying on top of a nearby box and began listlessly thumbing through the comic. Five minutes passed, then the door bell rang.

"You should probably get that," said Pointless Huck Finn.

"You think?" asked Larry. He shook his head. Sarcasm apparently had no effect on the dude. He returned to the front of the store and opened the door. A tall, gangly man in his early 20's flew past him, exhaling the odor of burnt corn silk. "Whoa, not so fast there, pal," he said. But Today's Tom Sawyer had already joined Pointless Huck Finn in the store room where, with many grunts and sighs, he commenced removing the boxes that stood above "1930's—Eight Pagers."

"If it's not too much to ask, do you think you might re-stack those boxes once you're finished?" asked Larry. The two ignored him. Finally, Today's Tom Sawyer lugged the box with the Depression-era porn comics across the floor. Huck and Tom began rooting through it, tossing books until they came to "Betty Boop Does Ming the Merciless."

"Sweet!" said Huck, whistling through his teeth. "Oh Betty, you naughty, dirty minx, you." He pressed the book to his lips.

"You going to buy that?" asked Larry. "Fifty bucks. And I'm taking a loss here."

Today's Tom Sawyer suddenly rose from the floor, pulled Larry to his chest and began vigorously sniffing him. "Huck has his pleasures," said Tom. "I have mine. Oh yeah, that's the primo bio-snuff."

"Got a good hit?" asked Huck.

"Hells yeah!" said Tom, relinquishing his grip on Larry. Larry fell back, dazed. He felt as though his life essence had been sucked. "What the fuck did you just do to me?" he asked, barely able to articulate the question.

"Today's Tom Sawyer, he gets high on you," said Pointless Huck Finn. "Okay, I'll take the book." He pulled a wad of cash from his jeans pocket and placed it in Larry's limp hands.

Larry watched as Pointless Huck Finn exited the store. Today's Tom Sawyer slid down beside him, a blissful grin on his face. "Since I started doing bio-snuff, my sex drive is less than zero," he said. "Hey, I'm really sorry about all this, man. Huck hasn't been the same since he lit out for the territories. When he came back, all he could talk about was vintage porno comics. Me, I've been a happy camper since I learned how to get high on people. It's greatest drug in the world. Don't worry, you'll recharge fully in about an hour or so."

"It's all good," said Larry. Thoroughly drained, he was also past caring. "You're all right, dude."

"Thanks," said Today's Tom Sawyer. "And here you are, my new friend. The Bangkok Gunfighter without Pointless Huck Finn. You want a hit off of me now?"

"Why fucking not?" said the Bangkok Gunfighter. "Why fucking not."

Mr. Sugar Comes to Splatterville

"How's business treating you, Mabel?" asked Gilbert Huncke. The retired 65-year-old publisher of the *Bunky's Folly Review* eased himself gingerly onto a stool behind the counter. The proprietress of Mabel's Pies slapped down a place setting in front of him and poured him a cup of coffee. "Oh, so-so," she said. He could hear the fatigue in her voice.

"Sure would be nice to have a slice of the your rhubarb," said Huncke, tossing two sugar packets into the coffee and stirring.

"Sure would be nice if you weren't such a jackass," said Mabel.

Huncke started. Mabel was famous for her attitude, but it mostly an act she put on for her long-time patrons. Now, she sounded genuinely mad.

She stabbed at the slate board hanging over the counter with her index finger. "See what it says?"

Huncke didn't have to read the menu. The yellow chalk letters hadn't changed for at least three years now: "Meat Only. No Substitutes."

"Oh hell, Mabel, I was just jokin' around. Gimme one of those pork pies."

Mabel sighed and swabbed the sweat from her forehead with a napkin. "I'm sorry, Gil. Didn't mean to snap at you. Guess it's just the strain. Things haven't been the same since..." Her voice trailed off.

"Know exactly what you mean," said Huncke. As if on cue, a teenage girl ran screaming through the front door followed swiftly by an ax-wielding man with long, ratty hair. The man raised the ax over his head and sank it into the girl's skull. She slumped to the scuffed linoleum floor. He stood over her and struck at her again and again until she was little more than hair, bones and shredded clumps of organ meat.

She nodded at the morbid mess. "Well, looks like I've got some mopping up to do."

Huncke stood up. "Here's a buck and change for the coffee," he said. "I seem to have lost my appetite for pie."

"Never you mind," said Mabel. "You know where to find it. Take care now." She sat on her haunches and began wearily to drop the larger chunks of girl into a plastic bucket. "Why can't they just do their business outside?" she grumbled to herself. "Well, no use complaining about spilled innards, I guess."

***

From the next town over, Shelby Sugar had seen Bucky's Folly gradually deteriorate. The candy scientist watched helplessly as middle American mores washed away in a tide of cannibalism, serial killing and random slaughter. Whether it was something in the water or the inevitable sequel to generations of inbreeding or the pernicious influence of popular culture with its internets and wi-fi's and iPod nanos, or liberal whackos with their mistaken belief in tolerance and inclusivity, Bucky's Folly no longer stood as a bastion of family values.

The new name, Splatterville, said it all. As long as chainsaws buzzed human limbs and pierced arteries spewed blood like high-pressure hoses, simple decency dropped her head for shame. Not only that, Sugar was a keen aficionado of Mabel's Pies from back in the day when wedges of lemon meringue, cherry, apple and pecan were served with a smile and a bit of sass. He would give anything for just one more piece of apple pie fresh from Mabel's oven, covered with a generous serving of vanilla ice cream. Finally, Sugar knew he had to take action, not only for the principle of the thing, but to keep the carnage from spreading any further.

As the scion of a dynasty devoted to confections, Mr. Sugar's knowledge base was limited. But he did understand the chemistry of candy and pastries, from bon bons and licorice whips to jelly rolls, eclairs and donuts; in the realm of sweets, his mastery was unrivaled. Moreover, gene-hacking was second nature to him, a talent passed down from his paternal grandfather. So, with a little reflection, he put two and two together and resolved on a plan.

The citizens of Splatterville reacted at first with skepticism to Sugar's ideas. "It's agin nature," said Jack Grungewort, the octogenarian Sheriff and Postmaster of Splatterville. Although Grungewort decried the plague of mayhem that had brought the town to its knees, Sugar's concepts seemed highly unorthodox to him, if not completely insane. Eventually, however, he yielded. He was sick of the whine of drills and the ooze of brain matter from freshly-bored heads, nostalgic for petty theft and disputes over lawn maintenance. "Go on," he told Sugar at last. "I suppose you couldn't make it any worse."

Starting his experiments on cadavers and proceeding to live subjects, Sugar began to infuse Splattervillians with new blood. Change came slowly, but as his methods became more sophisticated, Sugar succeeded in transforming the townsfolk into candy—licorice buttons for eyes, cherry-flavored gelatin for hearts, peppermint sticks for bones. In three months the old spirit had returned to the community; Splatterville was a happy place once more.

Not that the violence ceased in any substantial way, only it was fun now. Taffy guts were stretched from marshmallow stomachs with the victim's full consent and even participation. All the kids came running at the rumor of a slashing-in-progress. They eagerly swallowed fountains of red-dyed corn syrup and devoured the chocolate fundament of the hanged. Murder was now a taste everyone could share.

"My work here is done," said Mr. Sugar to Mabel, gratefully sinking his fork into a slice of her famous apple pie. "I'm going home."

Mabel's nougat features tinged with just a hint of cinnamon blush. "You dear man," she said, patting his hand. "Just don't forget about us, okay? And if you ever feel the craving, Mabel's is only a hop and a skip."

END.

Alex S. Johnson

Alex S. Johnson is the author of several books, including *Wicked Candy, Bad Sunset, Jason X IV: Death Moon* and *Outlaw Circus.* A former music journalist for such magazines as *Metal Hammer,* he currently lives in Sacramento, California, where he writes Bizarro horror and erotica stories and edits anthologies such as the *Axes of Evil* series and *Floppy Shoes Apocalypse,* a book of terrifying tales featuring clowns.

ALSO AVAILABLE FROM <u>MorbidbookS</u>
IN PRINT & KINDLE₁

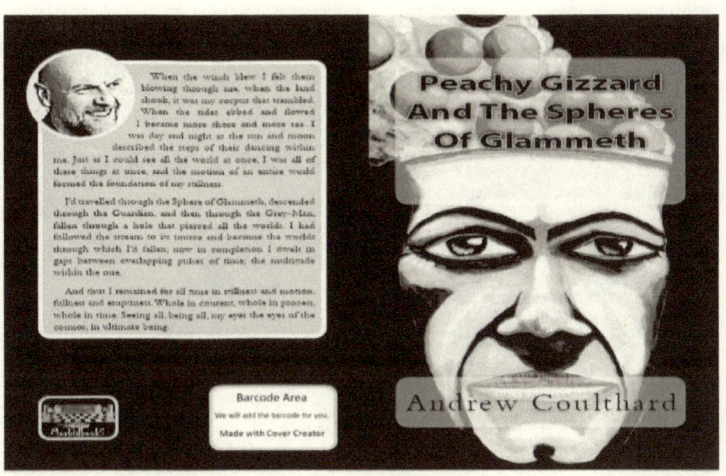

WHEN THE WINDS BLEW I FELT THEM BLOWING THROUGH ME,
when the land shook, it was my corpus that trembled. When the
tides ebbed and flowed I became more shore and more sea. I was
day and night as the sun and moon described the steps of their
dancing within me. Just as I could see all the world at once, I was
all of these things at once, and the motion of an entire world
formed the foundation of my stillness.

I'd travelled through the Sphere of Glammeth, descended through
the Guardian, and then through the Grey-Man, fallen through a
hole that pierced all the worlds. I had followed the stream to its
source and become the worlds through which I'd fallen; now in
completion I dwelt in gaps between overlapping pulses of time; the
multitude within the one.

And thus I remained for all time in stillness and motion, fullness
and emptiness. Whole in content, whole in process, whole in time.
Seeing all, being all, my eyes the eyes of the cosmos, in ultimate
being.

HE HAD TO HAVE HER THE MOMENT HE SAW HER TRACHEA RING. Six months later she was his lovely wife. He performed his duties as a husband and she as a wife. He tolerated a house filled with references to her late first husband and the children they had together. He put up with her prudish ways. He waited. He was patient. He planned. He was adaptable. He was rewarded over the course of a week in her basement. He turned his perverse sexual fantasies of worms and maggots and her lovely crusty trachea ring into a gruesome reality.

A DIRTY SHAMEFUL DEVIL OF A SECRET...

Something that two men share. A legacy that will shock you to your very core. One that is created not out of madness, but of the purest desire. Take a vivid journey into the mind of the killer and his biggest fan. Do you believe in evil? See the knife plunge. Lap at the wounds. Do you still? There is no rational meaning or pretty words that will hide away the darkness that the words of this found journal creates. Inside is the real truth. And it can set you free. Watch all you want. Taste what you dare not have. But once you see, you are in collusion. Keep reading and the guilt will stain. No longer can you feign innocence. The change is as permanent as it is wretched. Perhaps you should just walk away. This shit right here is a MorbidbookS blunt. You dig?

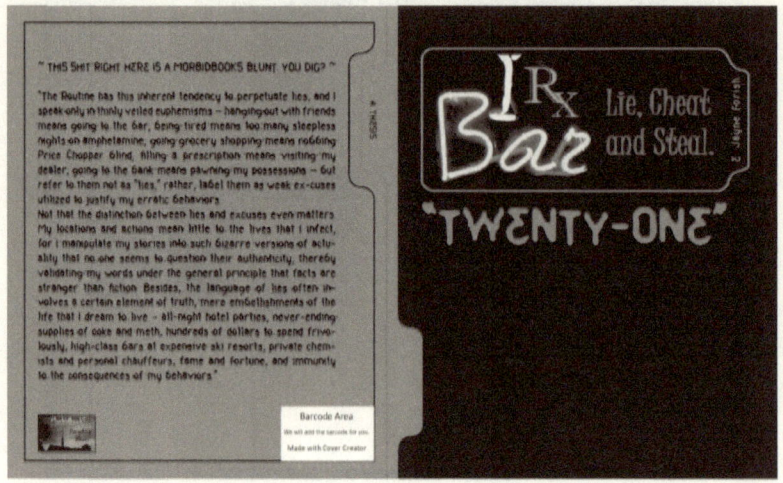

"THE ROUTINE HAS THIS INHERENT TENDENCY TO PERPETUATE LIES, and I speak only in thinly veiled euphemisms — hanging out with friends means going to the bar; being tired means too many sleepless nights on amphetamine; going grocery shopping means robbing Price Chopper blind; filling a prescription means visiting my dealer; going to the bank means pawning my possessions — but refer to them not as "lies;" rather, label them as weak excuses utilized to justify my erratic behaviors.

Not that the distinction between lies and excuses even matters. My locations and actions mean little to the lives that I infect, for I manipulate my stories into such bizarre versions of actuality that no one seems to question their authenticity, thereby validating my words under the general principle that facts are stranger than fiction. Besides, the language of lies often involves a certain element of truth, mere embellishments of the life that I dream to live – all–night hotel parties, never-ending supplies of coke and meth, hundreds of dollars to spend frivolously, high–class bars at expensive ski resorts, private chemists and personal chauffeurs, fame and fortune, and immunity to the consequences of my behaviors."

HUMANITY IS THE DEVIL IS A DECONSTRUCTED NIGHTMARE
mixing David Lynch and snuff movies. The plot revolves around a
central character, Seth, who is set about a crusade against
humanity which, for him, represents pure evil. Through random
killings he and his cronies try to accelerate the end of the world, in
order to provoke and defeat the Demiurge, the false God that is
ruling the earth. As in Burroughs, logical language is replaced here
with cut-scenes – sometimes to be taken literally – that plunge the
reader into an extreme experience. Both incredibly morbid and
enthralling, HITD is a masterpiece of moral darkness and
existentialist reflection upon our comfortable religion and morals.

Alex S. Johnson

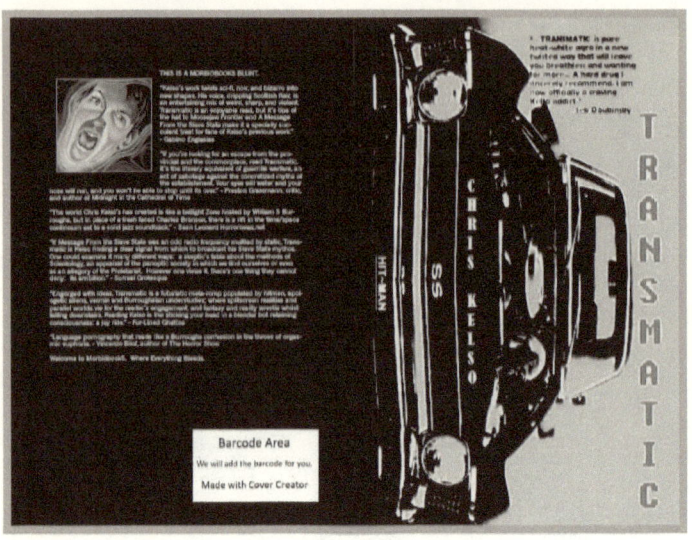

"AS A PART-TIME HITMAN/ EXTERMINATOR, Ignius Ellis's dream is to buy a candy-apple red Nova Supreme. In the process of trying to earn enough cash to make his dream come true he gets sucked into the rough world of Visitacion Valley, SF. When the tenants in his apartment complex reveal their various extracurricular activities this take an even more bizarre twist and Ellis soon becomes acquainted with the nightmarish Slave State dimension..."

THAT'S THE LAST TIME SHE GETS THE BIGGER WORM... Once their flesh flakes away the angels collapse into puddles of hissing goop and withered petals blow into them hurried along by unseen winds. My spit looses its sweet taste to the black flavor of ash. The glowing birds in the bright orange sky burst into small sparkly novas. The sky itself weeps and tears, streaking down like a ruined painting as the dismal gray of life wheezes back before my eyes. I don't blink; praying silently for one last desperate sensation of the high. Lila feels it too. She writhes on the mattress next to me; her moans of ecstasy warping into groans that capture the hollowness of our souls. Tears form in her eyes and I can almost feel the lump in her throat. It's gone and she wants to cry. I'd rather chase down more Worms than cry about it but everybody reacts to the Worms differently. I slip away to my own neon colored utopia where things with wings fan me and comfort me when the living neon worm dissolves under my skin. Lila told me once they wrap around her like a giant fuzzy neon hug. I imagine her high shedding off her like snake skin and flaking to the filthy floor next to the mattress. Her high sounds better than mine. More Fun. That's the last time she gets the bigger worm.

"IF YOU KNOW WHAT KINBAKU, POST-IMPRESSIONISM, and brilliant green eyes have in common, then you are probably a fan of Alex S. Johnson! Congrats! But if you don't know, allow me to open the door, guide you inside, and introduce you to a little Wicked Candy. This is a sweet designed for the discerning Bizarro fan's tastes, and I promise, you will not be disappointed!"
--Mimi Williams, author of Beautiful Monster

"A short collection that both traverses the genre lines and melds them together into one masterpiece. Jam packed with horror, laughs, pop culture history and more, this one is a must have for lovers of the macabre, the bizarre and the hilarious."
--Jeff O'Brien, author of Bigboobenstein

IN GARRETT COOK'S MURDERLAND serial killers are idolized by society. Their deeds are followed obsessively by television pundits and the adoring public. A subculture has grown up around this phenomena, called "Reap." Laws are created to allow this activity to flourish, including designated "safe zones' where killers can practice their trade without fear of persecution. Fans of the top rated serial killers celebrate each new kill on social media and television. Programs glorify their deeds.

The culture of Murderland is violent and mirrors our own violent society and its decadent obsessions; but Murderland isn't about how violent the world has become. It's about the pervasive nature of media and how it corrupts. It corrupts absolutely.

At the heart of Murderland is Jeremy Jenkins. Jeremy doesn't like what he sees and he's just enough insane to believe he can do something about it, that he can change the world. His methods are extreme– to outdo the serial killers, he'll kill THEM, turn their own twisted reality back on themselves. It's a hopeless task, impossible, Herculean; but it's Jeremy's fate to see it through to the-end.

The three sections of Murderland comprise a true Homeric epic. In the first section we are shown the terrible world Jeremy lives in, the world that if we look at it honestly, is really our own world. We meet all the principal characters, the serial killers, the pundits, the pawns, and Jeremy's beloved Cass. In the second section Jeremy goes on a bit of a spiritual quest and comes to understand his true purpose. In the final section the flames are ignited and all hell breaks loose. Jeremy, like a great epic hero must journey to the underworld and be reborn in order to triumph.

BORN WHOLE FROM THE RECTUM of a dying patient, Morbid silently stalks the hospital's hallways, heinously dispatching the most helpless of patients and in the most painfully repulsive of manners. In the meantime, in order to pay for his family and home that includes his ghost step-father Sammy and his pet aborted fetus Chip, Westphal has to ingest mounds of dangerous narcotics to get through his night shifts. Barely hanging on to his Care Tech gig by his fingernails, the last thing Westphal needs is to be accused of Morbid's evil deeds. You, on the other hand, simply want to find some solace. Terminally ill from a virulent infection, and dependent on Life Support, all You beg for a peaceful and dignified demise. Shirk has other plans for You. The ancient drug-snuffling demon makes You relive all of your deadly and venial sins as he tortures You. Night after night. Until eternal Damnation begins for YOU MORBID WESTPHAL, yet again.... NOW WITH EVEN *MORE* EVIL FLAVOR!

IT LOOKS LIKE CAROLYN AND MARK ARE IN DEEP, DEEP SHIT...

Mark and Carolyn live in an alternate 1989 where Ronald Reagan is on his fourth presidential term. The USA has a rigid, long-standing caste system and abortions were never made legal. Being homeless is a crime that is punishable by imprisonment in an internment camp the inmates call Tent City. Most of Mark's ER patients are inmates at this camp and are victims of a new disease these illegals call the Transient Flu. This deadly and rapidly spreading disease mutates with each new host, collecting information, changing code. The disease evolves lightning quick, spreading like pond ripples and infecting everyone. No one is safe. Mark and Carolyn dig too deep and uncover the brutal truth: Transient Flu was purposely made and is one hundred percent fatal. Carolyn's employer, Hudson-Smythe Pharmaceuticals, discovers the chain of evidence. It traces the pharmacide back to Hudson-Smythe and the crime of the century. Cost is no object and deadly force is authorized. Yes. Carolyn and Mark are in deep, deep shit.

IMMANUEL THE CHRIST HAS SOME NERVE. Jonah has already lost everyone he loves to Pilate the vampire and his Harbor drug violence. Jonah now trudges through his days staying as high on Plata as possible. He just wants to be left alone while he waits for his turn to die. The Christ has other plans for him. She sends Her messenger, Pedro, to assign Jonah the very dangerous task of ordering the Herod to dismantle the Harbor's Plata trade. Jonah decides to run. But you can't run from God forever. As Jonah learns the hard way when the 'Edmund Fitzgerald' founders and goes down in rough seas, with the reluctant prophet on board. Job is Satan's Chosen One and he doesn't take kindly to orders from some upstart prophet.

See Mo' Evil
Morbidbooks